"I'll be

Natalie

"Why are you being so stubborn about this. These girls need all the love they can get right now," Wyatt replied.

"Love, not more confusion."

Mr. Phillips's knuckles rapped softly on his desk. "While I respect how much you both care for the children, may I suggest that one of the best things you can do for them is present yourselves as a united front?"

Natalie let out a puff of air. "You're right."

"Of course," Wyatt agreed.

"Use the next few days to speak candidly about co-guardianship." Mr. Phillips pulled an official-looking sheet of paper from the file. "However, if you decide to send the girls to Forrest's cousin, let me know as soon as possible."

"Consider it done." Wyatt's eager tone got under Natalie's skin.

She hadn't felt this out of control in a long time.

But this wasn't about her. It was about Rose and Luna, even if it meant enduring a few days of forced proximity with the man who broke her heart.

Susanne Dietze began writing love stories in high school, casting her friends in the starring roles. Today, she's an award-winning, RWA RITA® Award–nominated author who's seen her work on the ECPA and *Publishers Weekly* bestseller lists for inspirational fiction. Married to a pastor and the mom of two, Susanne lives in California and enjoys fancy-schmancy tea parties, the beach and curling up on the couch with a costume drama. To learn more, say hi or sign up for her newsletter, visit her website, www.susannedietze.com.

Books by Susanne Dietze

Love Inspired

Home to Foxtail

Mountain Homecoming

Widow's Peak Creek

A Future for His Twins
Seeking Sanctuary
A Small-Town Christmas Challenge
A Need to Protect
The Secret Between Them

Love Inspired Historical

The Reluctant Guardian
A Mother for His Family

Visit the Author Profile page at LoveInspired.com.

MOUNTAIN HOMECOMING

SUSANNE DIETZE

LOVE INSPIRED

INSPIRATIONAL ROMANCE

LOVE INSPIRED®
INSPIRATIONAL ROMANCE

Recycling programs
for this product may
not exist in your area.

ISBN-13: 978-1-335-93728-5

Mountain Homecoming

Copyright © 2025 by Susanne Dietze

Love Inspired
22 Adelaide St. West, 41st Floor
Toronto, Ontario M5H 4E3, Canada
www.LoveInspired.com

Printed in Lithuania

MIX
Paper | Supporting
responsible forestry
FSC® C021394

Now faith is the substance of things hoped for,
the evidence of things not seen.
For by it the elders obtained a good report.
—*Hebrews* 11:1–2

To the Author of My Faith and Lifter of My Head

Acknowledgments

Many people helped me with various aspects of this book, and I am so grateful to each of them.

Thanks to authors Belle Calhoune, Jolene Navarro, Debra E. Marvin, Tina Radcliffe and Tanya Stowe for brainstorming help; Dr. Dan Stark for chatting with me about cedar trees; Karl, Hannah, Matthew, Mom and Dad for their love, support and company on an apple-picking adventure; and Darren Bogie, Susan Elliott and Jay Rosenlieb for answering my legal questions—any errors are mine alone, however.

I'm obliged to my editors, Amanda Sun, Melissa Endlich and Caroline Timmings, for helping me become a better writer, as well as to the entire Love Inspired team for their hard work publishing beautiful stories of faith, family and love. Thanks to my agent, Tamela Hancock Murray, for her prayers and generosity.

For as long as I live, I will cherish the love and sustaining prayers of precious friends, including the Daughters of the Holy Cross, Trinity Anglican Church, during a troubled time. Thank you, sisters. I am humbled by you, as I am by the faithfulness of the Lord, the Lover of my soul.

Chapter One

The moment he drove his truck past the pine-flanked sign welcoming him to Goldenrod, Wyatt Teague's stomach squeezed, as if he were bracing for a gut punch. He had missed his hometown in California's Cuyamaca Mountains the past nine months, but he'd had his reasons for staying away. Even though they confused and hurt the people he cared about.

One person in particular.

Shoving down the ache that always accompanied thoughts of Natalie Dalton, Wyatt took the fork left onto a curved, two-lane road, but there was little comfort in the familiar sights he passed—the cafés, the bed-and-breakfasts, the old white church, and winter-bare trees lining the road. All too soon, he turned right at a sign with the silhouette of a fox on it, a cheery font declaring he'd arrived at Foxtail Farm, a U-Pick apple orchard and tourist stop.

He pulled into the visitor parking lot, cut the ignition and stepped out of his truck. The gravel beneath his boots was still damp from the once-in-a-lifetime storm that roared through two days ago. A storm that caused a mudslide to sweep over the road into town at the exact moment his best friends, Forrest and Cady McHugh, were traveling home to their eight-month-old twin girls, Rose and Luna, after a date night.

Lord, I still can't believe Forrest and Cady are gone. The Bible says we don't grieve like those who have no hope, and I thank You for that. But—

No buts. He had hope, and it was high time he clung to it.

Stuffing his hands in the front pockets of his jeans, he strode across the empty parking lot toward the rustic wooden farm stand. Foxtail Farm hadn't suffered any ill effects from the torrential rain—that he could see, at least. The bare apple trees spread over several acres to his left. Bales of hay, barrels and a vintage John Deere tractor that kids could climb on for photo ops guided visitors toward the entrance of the house-size farm stand while allowing a line of sight into the shop. Inside, Wyatt knew there were bins of produce, baskets of flowers, gifts and rows of baked goods. Even from here, Wyatt could smell the cinnamon wafting from the bakery at the rear of the building.

But he wasn't here for one of Foxtail's famous apple pies.

He had an obligation to Forrest and Cady. A need to ensure their children were okay before they were claimed by their permanent guardians, whoever they were, since neither Forrest's nor Cady's parents were living. Natalie was temporary guardian of little Rose and Luna, so Wyatt would have to take a few lumps, seeing her, but he would keep his emotions in check. He had years of practice.

He took the path around the farm stand toward the family house, passing a grassy area with picnic tables, before entering a circular area of tall trees surrounding a stone fire pit and the rental cottage.

And his intentions to keep his emotions neutral evaporated like steam.

Because Natalie stood there, her back to him, pacing with her cell phone in hand alongside a barrier of yellow caution tape strung around Foxtail's rental cottage.

The white clapboard bungalow was a reliable source of income for Foxtail Farm—before their breakup, he and Natalie had been together so long that he knew a fair bit about Foxtail's financials. But the cottage was uninhabitable now, with that hundred-odd-foot uprooted incense cedar crashed atop the roof.

Oof, it was bad. The tree must have blown down in the storm. The yard-thick trunk lay sideways atop the cottage, while sprays of foliage and fragrant chunks of its fresh golden wood carpeted the ground. The cottage walls still stood, but he couldn't make out the chimney beneath the bright green branches splayed over the roof like bushy octopus tentacles.

Poor Natalie, facing a disaster like this on top of losing Cady and Forrest.

As much as he wanted to rush to her, he held back, letting her finish her tense-sounding conversation. Then she tapped the phone and shoved her hands into the center pocket of her sage hoodie sweatshirt, bowing her head as if in defeat.

"Natalie?"

She jumped and spun around, her dark eyes wide. "Mary Poppins!"

As in the fictional British nanny who floated down from the sky holding an umbrella? In the old days, he would have teased her, saying something like, *No, Nat, I know Mary and I look exactly alike, but I'm Wyatt.*

But they didn't have a relationship like that anymore. Other than her phone call to tell him about Forrest and Cady's accident, they hadn't spoken since he left.

He took a tentative step forward. "Sorry, I didn't mean to startle you."

"It's okay. I'm just preoccupied." Color bloomed in her cheeks. "And I didn't hear you coming."

He had never been accused of being subtle, not at his lumbering size, but her phone conversation had clearly been intense.

A stiff gust of the cold January breeze ruffled the dark hair she'd bound in a high ponytail, and he couldn't help but recall how he used to twine strands of her silken hair around his fingers.

Knock it off, Teague. Stick to safe topics.

Like the tree on top of the cottage. His stance widened as he dropped into work mode to survey the damage. "This is awful. Was anyone hurt?"

"No, thankfully. Winter bookings are few and far between. As you may remember." There was a tinge of acid in the last bit, but he hadn't forgotten. Once, he'd shared her vision of making Foxtail Farm a year-round destination for families. That dream had crumbled like the cottage roof, though. She turned back to the damage with a sigh. "I love this cottage."

"I know, but I can see some potential dangers from a safety standpoint— Sorry." He held up his hands, acknowledging she didn't require his expertise as an architect and builder. "That's not what you need to hear right now."

"No, but you're not wrong. I just got off the phone with the insurance agent. A crew is coming tomorrow morning at seven to retrieve what's salvageable from inside and then demolish the cottage." Her voice wavered, but before he could attempt to offer any words of comfort, she lifted her chin. "I didn't expect to see you for a few hours. Downtown."

They had an appointment with Forrest and Cady's lawyer. Years ago, Wyatt had agreed to be the executor of Forrest's estate should tragedy arise, but he'd never expected to serve in that capacity. Not for several decades, at least.

The message the lawyer left on Wyatt's voicemail informed him Natalie would be at the meeting, too. Wyatt suspected the three of them would go over transfer of the babies to their new guardians. But that appointment wasn't the only reason he'd returned to Goldenrod. "Where are Rose and Luna?"

"At the house." She hitched her thumb behind her, in the direction of the Dalton family home, which at some point had been divided into four separate living quarters. At present, the other three apartments were occupied by her younger sisters, Sadie and Dove, and their cousin Thatcher, who was days younger than Natalie.

"I'd like to see them."

"Why?"

A simple question, but it was loaded. "Are you serious?"

"I'm too tired and sad to be anything else, Wyatt."

"I care about them."

Her eyes were wide with disbelief. "But you've never even seen them, because you left before they were born."

"That's not true. I've seen them several times. They stayed at my place New Year's Eve." Three weeks ago. The girls had adored the holiday lights festival they'd attended.

"I knew they went out of town for New Year's, but Cady didn't say it was to see you." She blinked, as if she felt betrayed by their friends visiting him.

If that was what she thought, then he needed to put that idea to rest. "Probably because they didn't want to stir up any unhappy memories. They didn't take sides between us, honest. Cady was your best friend, but Forrest was mine, and Rose and Luna are his children, too. If it had been physically possible, I would have left Irvine for Goldenrod the minute you called about the accident, but Caltrans didn't finish clearing the mudslide off the road until early this morning. So here I am."

She chewed her lip, deliberating, and he understood why she was hesitant. Their engagement had ended badly. He hadn't been back to town since, not even to visit his parents. But he'd never ceased caring for Forrest and Cady. Never stopped caring for anyone.

Even her, despite how things ended.

She sighed. "The girls are probably still asleep."

"I won't make a sound. I'll tiptoe and everything."

"In those size-twenty boots you clomp around in? Ha."

At her joke exaggerating the size of his admittedly large feet, he couldn't help the twitch at his lips. "Is that a yes?"

"Yes, because I know you're grieving, and I would like to see the girls, too."

It sounded like a *but* was coming, but instead she stomped past him up the tree-lined path to the family's private quarters. Within seconds, they cleared the trees and strode up a narrow cement walk bisecting the lawn to the white ranch-style house. Pruned rosebushes, resting for the winter among evergreen shrubs, fronted the brick foundation and flanked the three creaky steps to the wraparound porch where they used to watch the sunset, cuddled together on the double glider.

Before he'd made the biggest mistake of his life—which he was not going to think about now.

Without a glance, Natalie led him through the foyer to the first door on the right—her quarters. He crossed the threshold and blinked. Twice.

The snug apartment had always been tidy, an extension of Natalie's personality, but he could hardly make out the cream-colored sofa, driftwood coffee table or gray patterned rug beneath all the baby paraphernalia—pastel blankets, toys, a bouncy-looking seat contraption and an overflowing laundry basket. If lavender was still her signature fragrance, it was buried beneath the distinct smells of oat cereal and brewing coffee.

"Wow—sorry." He'd forgotten to whisper.

"I've been a little busy." Her whisper was strained. "The babies aren't sleeping, and no wonder. They miss their parents."

"I didn't mean it as a criticism, Nat. You've been working hard taking care of them, that's obvious." He might have said more, but what good would it do? He was fumbling here. He turned to shut the door behind him as softly as he could so as not to make any more noise.

"Wyatt Teague, I do declare." A hushed alto voice drew him around.

Beatie and Dutch Underhill, the sixtysomething couple who had managed the apple orchard for decades, appeared from behind the partitioned kitchen wall. He hadn't realized until this moment how much he had missed them: Dutch, with his tuft of faded red hair atop his head and deeply wrinkled brow, and Beatie, her silver-gilt hair cascading in waves down her shoulders and over her eggplant-hued sweatshirt as she smiled at him with genuine affection.

Wyatt met Beatie halfway for one of her famous bear hugs. "Good to see you. Just wish it weren't under these circumstances."

Beatie's eyes were moist when she stepped back. "Cady and Forrest were good people. I remember when you two were the maid of honor and best man at their wedding. Such bright futures ahead of them. How could this have happened?"

"I'm still in shock. I'm sure we all are." Wyatt exchanged a firm handshake with Dutch.

The older man held on a moment longer than necessary. "Shock and sadness, but we can't forget that we're all in this together."

"Which means any differences of opinion you two have must be set aside, pronto." Beatie's thick eyebrows drew into a stern expression. "Bickering isn't good for the babies."

Dutch's lips quirked. "Subtle as a boulder, woman."

"Someone needs to say it like it is." Beatie shrugged.

Hint taken, but Wyatt wouldn't be here long. "Speaking of the babies?" Wyatt tipped his head at Natalie.

"In the bedroom."

Wyatt slipped into the small chamber, dimly illuminated by weak winter sunlight. A double bed spread with a quilt the color of sea glass took up most of the space, and a portable crib filled a corner. He crept up to it, afraid to breathe lest he make a noise and wake its sleeping occupants.

Rose and Luna lay side by side, their tiny fists flung above their heads, long lashes fanning round, pink cheeks. Both girls had inherited their dad's strawberry-blond hair, but smaller Rose still didn't have more than a downy fuzz atop her head. Luna's hair, however, curled like a Kewpie doll's over her forehead.

My girls, Forrest used to say.

Forever your girls, Wyatt wished he could say to his best friend. A lump of grief hardened in his throat, and instinctively, he swallowed it down.

God, please protect these little ones. May they never know a single day unaware of how much their mom and dad loved them.

Would their guardians tell them? Share stories about their parents, show them pictures? Wyatt exhaled and released his concern to God. He would trust Him to care for Rose and Luna, wherever that took them.

Even though the thought of never seeing them again made his stomach feel like it was twisting inside out.

"Well, *this* is a surprise," Beatie whispered as she pointed at the wall dividing them from Wyatt and the babies. "Did you know he was coming?"

"No. Not to Foxtail, anyway. I knew we'd see each other at the law office." By which time Natalie had planned to be showered, changed out of her spit-up–splotched sweatshirt and mentally prepared to face him.

So much for that.

She sat on the couch and pulled the plastic laundry basket toward her, retrieving a pair of footed pajamas to fold. "He'll probably be gone in fifteen minutes, tops."

"What did you hear from the insurance company?" Dutch settled his lanky frame into a chair.

While she gave them a summary of the sad news about the cottage's demolition, her mind returned to concerns about how she would get everything done. Although her family and friends had pitched in for short stretches, Natalie was the girls' temporary guardian, a role she was honored to play, but she was weary. The girls were understandably fussy, and Natalie hadn't slept much, nor been able to see to her duties at Foxtail, since the accident.

Back when she was still on the phone with the insurance agent, she had entertained the briefest fantasy about Mary Poppins floating down from the overcast sky to lend a hand with Rose and Luna.

But instead, she'd been startled by the six-foot-two lumberjack of a man who had broken her heart.

Wyatt Teague. Any comparison between the fictional

nanny and Wyatt was laughable, except for the whole thing about adding fun to whatever task needed doing. Wyatt and Mary would get along great there. But still.

When I asked for help, Lord? I didn't mean him.

It annoyed her that she'd blurted out the words *Mary Poppins* when she saw him. It was almost as annoying as the fact that Wyatt was still knee-wobblingly handsome, with those loose gold-brown curls she used to run her fingers through. He wore faded jeans and a jade-and-cream-plaid flannel shirt rolled up to reveal corded wrists. She'd always loved that shirt, which made his surf-green eyes pop.

What she didn't love was the way seeing him for the first time in nine months reduced her leg bones to apple butter, even after all they'd been through.

Pathetic.

Wyatt wasn't a bad guy. She wouldn't have accepted his marriage proposal if he had been. But no matter how many good qualities he had, he'd left when she'd needed him most.

Beatie sat beside her. "Honey, I'm so sorry about the cottage. What a blow."

Emotionally as well as professionally. "The walls are still standing. I truly thought once the cedar was removed, cosmetic repairs would be all the cottage required."

"Looks can be deceiving." Beatie pulled a clean crib sheet from the basket to fold. "Some things can't be patched up and painted over. They have to be rebuilt from the foundation up."

Dutch joined in the folding, selecting a baby washcloth. "Insurance will cover the cost of rebuilding the cottage, but it could be a while before the new one is ready."

A realization pinched at her. "The wedding in April. It can't happen now."

Beatie tutted. "Sure, it can. That cute couple wants their ceremony in the orchard. It's fine there."

"Yes, but they chose Foxtail because of the cottage. The bride's family wanted to stay at the site of the ceremony to better accommodate a relative with mobility issues, which I completely understand." Natalie pulled her phone from her jeans pocket and added the item to her long to-do list. "Once I tell them that's no longer possible here, I expect they'll get married at another orchard."

"That's disappointing." Dutch let out a resigned breath. "You've worked so hard to get the farm's finances in the black, Natalie. You and the others."

She, Sadie, Dove and Thatcher ran Foxtail Farm, each managing a specific component of the farm's enterprises— the farm stand gift shop, bakery, hobby cattle ranch and, in Natalie's case, the main office—precisely as Natalie's late father, Asa Dalton, had specified in his will. And they had to follow Asa's instructions for five long years (*one down, four to go*, they were fond of reminding each other) or all four of them would lose their inheritances. The farm would be sold, and employees like Dutch and Beatie would lose their jobs.

Talk about a heavy incentive to toe the line.

"You'll think of something, honey." Beatie patted her arm. "You always do."

Out of necessity. *Typical oldest child, keeping everything organized*, her mom liked to say. Frankly, Natalie viewed the characteristic as less of a birth order trait and more of a requirement, considering her upbringing shuttling between her frustrated mother and her irresponsible dad. His stringent last will and testament was completely out of his character.

Between last year's drought and poor apple harvest, and

now no possibility of income from the cottage, she wasn't sure how the farm would make it through the new year.

God, we need You. Following Him was new to Natalie, but she knew He was worthy of trust.

Her phone pinged, and the name of Forrest and Cady's lawyer appeared on the screen, with a text addressed to her and Wyatt. Before she could open the text, Wyatt slipped from the bedroom, holding his phone. "What do you think? Can you make it work?"

She skimmed the message, then looked at Beatie and Dutch. "The lawyer wants to meet us right now, if possible. The storm caused a landslide on his property, and his schedule for the day needs to shift to accommodate an inspection. Something about storm damage to his house." She wouldn't have time to change clothes, but the prospect of getting this over with and not seeing Wyatt again until the funeral on Saturday held appeal. "Would you be able to stay for a while longer? Sadie is making floral deliveries and Dove is with a vendor. Even Thatcher is busy repairing that section of fence."

"I'm not sure that cousin of yours would know what to do with a diaper, anyway." Beatie shooed them with her hands. "Silas—you remember the new hire? He has the pruning in hand. We can stay with these little darlings as long as you need."

Wyatt bent to clap Dutch's shoulder and kiss Beatie's cheek. "See you at the service." Then he turned to Natalie. "Care to ride with me? The truck is parked at the farm stand."

"Actually, I need to pick up formula while I'm out." Natalie scooped up her purse. She knew he would have been happy to stop by the store for her, but being alone with him seemed like too much right now. "See you there."

The law office of Phillips & Kim was a few streets from the touristy main drag, and within minutes she was seated beside Wyatt in one of two padded chairs before the lawyer's desk.

"Thanks for coming at such short notice." Craig Phillips, a balding man in his midfifties, pushed his silver-rimmed glasses higher up his nose. "My back patio is built on a slope. *Was*, I should say. There's concern about the house sliding down, too."

Wyatt winced. "That's a frightening situation."

"Indeed, but losing a house is a trifle compared to the loss of friends. My condolences. How are the children doing?"

"Physically, they're fine, but they're confused." Grief surged through her. "They have a rough adjustment ahead."

"Agreed, so let's get them settled as quickly as possible." Mr. Phillips retrieved a folder from a stack at his side. "You both should have copies of their recent will."

"I wouldn't call it recent. It's five, six years old." Wyatt glanced at Natalie.

She shook her head. "Cady never gave me any papers."

The lawyer's shiny brow puckered. "You approved the terms, however, didn't you?"

"I don't know what you're talking about." Anxiety tightened Natalie's throat like a purse string. "Wyatt?"

"I don't know." His hand landed on her forearm, a gentle touch that soothed her more than she would dare admit. "Clearly, we're in the dark here."

The lawyer frowned. "Forrest and Cady updated their will almost a year ago. They chose you both to care for their unborn children, should they be rendered incapable." He pulled papers from the pile and slid them across the desk.

Natalie stumbled over the full meaning of the lawyer's words.

You both. Her and Wyatt. Together.
That was impossible. Intolerable.
She had to find a way out of this, and fast.

Chapter Two

Adrenaline pumped hot and fast through her veins as Natalie stared at the guardianship clause of the will. Surely there was a way out.

But after scanning the section four times, she saw nothing ambiguous in the legal document.

Cady and Forrest had updated their will three months before Rose and Luna arrived, but they hadn't thought to change it after Wyatt drove off in his truck and Natalie shoved her engagement ring in a box at the back of her sock drawer. An oversight, probably, but what a mess.

Meanwhile, the lawyer watched them, his brow furrowed. "I regret that this comes as such a shock, but I did inform you, Miss Dalton. I mentioned the guardianship when I phoned you the other day."

"You used the word *temporary*. I thought I had been named to care for the girls until their permanent situation was finalized."

"Finalized with the *judge*, not other guardians." Mr. Phillips leaned forward. "Is there a problem?"

"First things first." Wyatt's cheeks had lost their usual ruddiness, a sure sign he was as shocked as she was about this. "Forrest and Cady never asked me to serve as a guardian, and it sounds like they didn't ask Natalie, either. Is it legal to name guardians without their knowledge?"

Mr. Phillips's hand curved up in an ambiguous gesture. "It's unexpected, but there is nothing illegal in it, no."

"Another thing." Natalie glanced at her ringless left hand. "When they drew up this will, Wyatt and I planned to be married, but we aren't engaged anymore. I assume that changes things."

"Your relationship or lack thereof isn't a condition of the will. The court's concern will be whether the children are safe, loved and nurtured, now and through the years to come."

A lifetime commitment to the girls didn't scare Natalie. But the thought of sharing them with Wyatt until they were eighteen, at the very least?

It was enough to send her into a panic attack.

She scrambled for an idea. "Can I...do this alone?"

Wyatt's brows pulled low in disbelief. "You want to cut me out?"

"It's practical, not personal." Well, it was both, but she wouldn't get into that here. "You live a two-and-a-half-hour drive away, without rush-hour traffic."

"I don't need to live in Goldenrod to make this work." A vein bulged in his temple.

"Before you go any further, allow me to draw your attention to the next page." Mr. Phillips flipped over the top sheet of the will, revealing a continuation to the guardianship clause. "It states that if one of you is unwilling to raise the children at the time they come to you, the girls should go to Forrest's cousin."

"Hendrick and Gwyneth." Natalie bit her lip. She'd heard about them.

Wyatt glanced at her. "Since they are pretty much the

only family Forrest or Cady had, I expected the girls to go to them in the first place."

Mr. Phillips looked stoic, but she could read disapproval in his eyes. "I can reach out to them, if you prefer that arrangement."

Natalie held up a hand. "That's not what we're saying. At least, it's not what *I'm* saying. This is so much, so fast. Are we allowed a few days to figure things out? Hendrick and Gwyneth aren't available right now, anyway. When I contacted them about the accident, they were on a remote hiking vacation, about to enter an area without cell reception. They said they'd be at the funeral on Saturday, though."

She didn't intend for her words to sound disparaging, but Hendrick had seemed far more concerned about how long their conversation would hold up the hiking group than the fact that he'd lost his cousin in a terrible accident. And he never asked about the girls.

Mr. Phillips took a sharp, whistling breath. "Perhaps you could discuss the matter with them around the funeral?"

"That sounds good," Wyatt said with a nod. "I'll be there to help."

Natalie couldn't stop herself. "That's not necessary."

"Why are you being so stubborn about this? Those girls need all the love they can get right now."

"Love, not more confusion."

Mr. Phillips's knuckles rapped softly on his desk. "I can't imagine how devastating this time must be for you both. While I respect how much you both care for the children, may I suggest that one of the best things you can do for them is present yourselves as a united front?"

Natalie let out a puff of air. "You're right."

"Of course," Wyatt agreed.

"Use the next few days to speak candidly about co-guardianship." Mr. Phillips pulled an official-looking sheet of paper from the file and passed it across the table. "Here's a list of what to expect if you choose to go forward—observation by a court-appointed investigator and a hearing in two months' time with a judge, probably at the courthouse in El Cajon. However, if you decide to send the girls to Forrest's cousin, let me know as soon as possible."

"Consider it done." Wyatt's eager tone got under Natalie's skin. "But it would be far easier for me to do my part caring for Rose and Luna if I lived with them."

"You want to take the girls back to Irvine?" Natalie would have thought she'd had enough big surprises today, but this iced the cake. "No way."

"I'm suggesting Rose and Luna move back to Forrest and Cady's house, where everything is familiar to them. You and I can take turns staying overnight with them."

"Oh." Reluctant as she was to admit it, his idea did sound better for the babies. They would be more comfortable there, with their possessions, beds, and even a full bathtub rather than the kitchen sink. And it was definitely less cramped than Natalie's apartment.

But it still wasn't feasible. "I can't stay at their place. Dad's will stipulates I reside on Foxtail property."

The lawyer rubbed his chin. "As your father's attorney, I am well acquainted with the caveats of his will. However, I'm confident that alternate evenings at the McHugh home will not violate your father's terms."

Natalie let out her breath. She hadn't felt this out of control in a long time.

But this wasn't about her. It was about Rose and Luna, even if it meant enduring a few days of forced proximity with the man who broke her heart.

She had been attending church for half a year now but

still struggled with believing God was with her every step of the way. Maybe it was hard to trust her Heavenly Father because her earthly one had been so unreliable. Regardless, here was an opportunity to walk in faith, not by sight.

Even though she didn't want to do that walking—even for a few days—alongside the likes of Wyatt Teague.

After an afternoon of Baby Care Boot Camp with Natalie and Beatie—diapers, bottles and laundry he almost ruined by adding regular detergent instead of delicate baby soap—Wyatt sat at Natalie's small kitchen table, holding a spoon mounded with soft-cooked butternut squash. "Ready, Luna?"

Luna, secured in a clip-on high chair, accepted the spoonful. Then a second and third. Feeding babies was easy.

Until he looked at Rose, wriggling on Natalie's lap, as if there were more interesting things in the world to do than eat. Meanwhile he—and Natalie, he was sure—wanted nothing more than to wolf down their dinners, too. This was the first opportunity he'd had to sit at the table since Natalie's sisters brought over a hot casserole after Beatie and Dutch left. The casserole had gone cold before he and Natalie could touch it, but at last they had plates of reheated food. Natalie ignored hers, focusing on feeding Rose.

Wyatt didn't intend to heat up his food a second time. While Luna took a break to watch Natalie's sisters in the kitchen, he scooped himself a forkful of poppy seed chicken and rice, one of his favorite comfort foods. Oh, man, that tasted good, creamy and filling. Then he scraped up another spoonful of squash and lifted it to Luna's lips. "Your turn, Lu-lu."

She opened her mouth like a cute baby bird. Smiled.

And then spat it out with a *pffft*. Bright orange stuff shot down her chin and spattered the table.

"No, Luna. Swallow." Wyatt scooped the excess off the baby's chin with the spoon.

"Wyatt, would you please pass the pepper?"

"Sure. Here you go."

How polite they sounded. Excessively so, since returning from the lawyer's office. He had felt convicted by Mr. Phillips's admonition to present a united front to the girls, but he knew Natalie was struggling as much as he was. They were grieving, shell-shocked, confused and uncertain about what to do for the long haul. Clearly, she didn't want to raise the girls with him, but didn't she want to honor Forrest and Cady's wishes?

By mutual decision, however, they had decided not to talk about it tonight. Nor would they move the girls back home until tomorrow morning. It was too much work, and they were both exhausted. So here they were, being nice and courteous while they cared for the babies.

Did her sisters notice that it masked the tension between them? Perhaps they were too busy. Dove, the baby in Natalie's family, served up pie while Sadie, the middle-born sister, put away the dishes she had just dried.

"Eat those num-nums, Luna." Dove, a rounder, blonder version of Natalie, smiled at the baby and set a wedge of Foxtail's famous pie on the edge of his place mat. The delectable fragrances of cinnamon and apples made his mouth water.

He glanced up at her. "No one bakes pie like you, Dove."

"That's why they pay me the big bucks in the bakery." She laughed at her own joke before placing a second piece at Natalie's elbow. "This is day-old, so don't get too excited. Since the storm, we haven't had many customers at the farm stand."

Little wonder. The locals were knee-deep in mourning or cleaning storm damage, and tourists hadn't been able to come into town since the mudslide. A damper fell over them.

Luna's impatient squawk broke the tension, making Wyatt chuckle. "Am I too slow?"

"Mm-gff-mm." Luna accepted her next bite eagerly, but at the same time, she spread her pudgy hands over the table, finger-painting with the spilled squash.

"No, Luna. Here."

Too late. Before he could wipe her pudgy fingers, she patted her curly head. "Ubba-do," she announced.

He didn't speak baby, but he could tell she enjoyed the feeling of slimy squash between her fingers. He grabbed a rag and enveloped her tiny, dimpled hands in it. "Ubba-do back atcha, and now there's squash all over you."

"And you, Wyatt." Dove pointed at his shirt.

He hadn't noticed the orange spatter across his chest. "It'll wash."

"So will these girls." Sadie, taller and blonder than her sisters, grinned at Luna. "Shall I go ahead and fill the sink for their baths?"

"Please." Natalie wiped Rose's chin with her terry-cloth bib. "There aren't any tubs in the house. Just showers," she explained to Wyatt.

"My mom bathed us in the sink when we were little. There are loads of embarrassing photos to prove it." Including a framed snap, hung in the hallway, of Wyatt and his same-aged cousin, Mick, when they were about the same age as Rose and Luna. Wyatt pointed his fork at her plate. "While Rose gets cleaned up, you can eat."

She stood and handed Rose to Dove. "Actually, I can take over with Luna and you can go on to your parents' house, if you want."

Was she trying to get rid of him, or being polite? "My folks know I'm staying here until the babies go down for the night."

Sadie ran the water, and the kitchen filled with the scent of lavender-tinged soap, along with the homey sounds of forks on plates, Luna's gurgles as she finished her squash and a happy squeal when Rose was lowered into the warm water. Nevertheless, everything felt stilted. Off.

As if they were all too aware nothing was how it should be, without Forrest or Cady. With Wyatt here instead.

He had expected awkwardness with Sadie and Dove, but if they were upset with him over the breakup with Natalie, they hadn't shown it. The babies seemed to be everyone's top priority.

He was grateful, although he deserved their disapproval for hurting Natalie. That had never been his intention in following his architectural firm out of the county. In fact, he'd expected the rough spots between them to eventually buff out like the spilled squash he swiped from the table with the rag once Luna was finished.

At least he'd successfully protected Natalie from learning he was not the man she thought he was. How badly he'd failed her.

He never wanted her to know the truth, and if he left town as planned after the funeral, his secret would be safe. But Forrest and Cady's will had thrown a wrench in his plans. *God, what's best for Rose and Luna?*

An answer would come, he was sure of it, but in the meantime, he had a God-given task in front of him: meeting these babies' immediate needs.

Sadie lifted Rose from the sink and quickly bundled her in a yellow towel with a hood that looked like a ducky face. "Who wants to put her in her jammies while I bathe Luna?"

"I'm done eating." Wyatt hopped up and took the toweled baby in his arms, carrying her into the living room.

Natalie had created a makeshift changing station on the floor by placing a beach towel atop the plush rug, setting out clean diapers and pajamas for the girls. He quickly dried and diapered Rose, then gently guided her arms and one leg into the footed pajamas. The second leg, however, pumped like she was in a bicycle race.

Should he just grab her leg and stick it in the pajamas? He didn't want to hurt her. He knew how much pressure to exert with a sledgehammer. A jackhammer. A regular hammer. But a hammering baby leg? "Rose, don't you want to be warm in your cozy pj's?"

Apparently not. She giggled, revealing two tiny bottom teeth.

"Tell you what. If you lie still until I snap you up, then I get another piece of pie and you can lick the spoon."

"Rose, tell Wyatt babies don't eat pie." Natalie entered the living room, carrying her plate of dessert.

He liked this sort of talk far better than the extreme politeness, so he followed her lead and teasingly talked to her through Rose. "Rose, tell Natalie you plan on eating a lot of Dove's pies once you get more teeth."

"Mm-gmm," Rose said.

"See? She's on board." He tried again with the pajama leg and failed.

"Need a hand?"

It was an innocent-sounding question, but Wyatt's guard went up. He was a thirty-one-year-old man losing the pajama war against an eight-month-old. Was she silently judging him, wanting to take over?

He may have made some poor choices in the past, but he had no intention of being hands-off with Forrest's kids. "Nah, we've got this. Don't we, Rose?"

The baby rolled onto her stomach.

Wyatt laughed. "You've got spunk, kid, that's for sure." Rather than turn the baby over on her back, he tugged the pajama leg down and over Rose's toes, then fastened the snaps beneath her before she had a chance to kick out of it. "Bingo."

Natalie's front door swung open without so much as a knock. A thirtyish man charged into the living room, silent in his stocking feet. Thatcher Dalton, Natalie's cousin, must have taken his work boots off on the porch, but he still smelled of cattle. He wore jeans, a thick flannel jacket and a wide grin that died when he caught sight of Wyatt on the floor.

"You."

"Evenin', Thatcher." Rising, Wyatt scooped up Rose.

Dove came out from the kitchen, a bottle of milk in her hand, followed by Sadie with Luna, bundled in an orange towel with a fox face on the hood.

Natalie reached for the fresh-bathed baby. "I'll get this little one in her jammies."

"And you and I can catch up for a minute, Teague. Outside." Thatcher glared at Wyatt, but his gaze softened a fraction when he realized Rose was in Wyatt's arms. "You might want to put the baby down for this."

Wyatt handed Rose to a stunned-looking Sadie. "Be right back, ladies." He followed Thatcher out through the foyer and onto the dimly lit porch.

Thatcher's thick finger was immediately in Wyatt's face.

"Look, I don't know what happened between you and Natalie. None of us do. But if you hurt her again, I can't guarantee I won't do something regrettable."

Wyatt didn't flinch. Thatcher might be an inch taller than he, brawny from ranch work, but Wyatt could take whatever his old friend dished out. "I would deserve it, too. For what it's worth, the last thing I want to do is cause her pain."

"Good answer." Thatcher's finger fell. "Maybe I'm coming on strong, but I'm the closest thing Natalie has to a brother. I would hate for her to get her heart broken again."

"She won't. Not on my account." Wyatt held up his hands in a gesture of surrender. "I'm glad she has you to look out for her."

Thatcher looked like he had more questions, but then he shifted to lean against the porch railing. With his dark hair and chiseled features, he looked like Natalie's dad's side of the family. "I missed you, man."

"I missed you, too."

"So, what happens now? Are you staying in town?"

"I don't know." He gave a brief rundown of their time with the lawyer.

"You're giving up the girls to the cousin?" Disbelief widened Thatcher's eyes.

"It might be what's best for the girls, and I don't live in town. Our options are limited, but... I don't know. We need to discuss it."

Thatcher shook his head. "Well, Forrest and Cady put their trust in you. As long as you make the best decision you can for the babies and for Natalie, I'll trust you, too. But now let's get back inside. My feet are freezing."

Inside, Dove was offering Rose a bottle while Natalie fed Luna. Soft instrumental music played from Natalie's phone, and the lights were dimmed. Things were winding down for bedtime.

Thatcher tiptoed to the couch and sat down, and as quietly as he could, Wyatt started gathering up toys and stacking them in a cloth basket. It had to be done before they moved them to the McHughs' house tomorrow, anyway.

He looked over at Natalie. He wished he weren't taken captive by the way her dark hair fell over her shoulder, mirroring the curve of her cheek. Even though her features were lined with fatigue, she was still the loveliest woman he'd ever seen. Ever would see. How could he not wish things had turned out differently between them? The unexpected tempests of life cut their relationship to the quick as surely as the recent storm uprooted that incense cedar.

The tree reminded him. "Nat?" His voice was low. "Tomorrow morning, when the demo crew comes? I can handle that for you."

"You don't need to do that. It'll be early."

"Yeah, and there's a good chance you'll have been up in the night with the girls. I can take them if you'd prefer, but if I meet the crew instead, you can have a slower morning. Besides, it would spare you having to witness the demolition."

Thatcher gave him a discreet thumbs-up.

Natalie chewed her lip, then nodded. "I was dreading having to watch it come down. Thank you."

"I'm happy to." It wasn't much of a gesture, but it was a start. He didn't have much else to offer her, other than prayers, and he would start with those now. For rest, healing, peace, for her burdens to lift. It sounded like Foxtail's finances weren't in any better shape than they'd been when he left, and the future wasn't looking so hot now that the cottage was coming down.

Unless there was somewhere else for paying guests to stay...

An idea raced through his head. It was a long shot, but he had to give it a try.

He could never make up for hurting her, but he could try to make her life a little better since he'd made such a mess of things.

Chapter Three

Once Rose and Luna were asleep in their cribs, there was no reason for Wyatt to stay at Natalie's. He said good night, and within ten minutes, his truck's headlights lit up the border fence of Manzanita Ranch, the horse ranch where he'd been raised.

He passed the driveway to his parents' house and pulled into the ranch's work entrance, circling the stables for the boarded horses and breeding mares. He parked behind the smallest stable, the one that housed the family's personal horses.

He pulled out his phone, opened his contacts and tapped out a quick message.

Hey, Alex. Made it through the day. Thanks for the prayers.

Right away, three dots appeared on the screen. Wyatt waited a few seconds before the response came through.

Keep leaning on His strength. Talk tomorrow.

God's strength...boy, did Wyatt need it.

He pocketed his phone and looked through the windshield at the stable. Light streamed through the high windows. One of the hired hands must be finishing up chores inside. Wyatt wouldn't get in the way. This would only take a minute.

He slipped inside, at once comforted by the smells of hay, horse and feed. To his surprise, a frosted-faced chocolate Labrador sat in the aisleway, alongside a dark-haired man in a gray quilted jacket. No employee. "Mick! What are you doing out here?"

"I could ask you the same thing, man. Good to see you." His maternal cousin met him halfway for a hug, thumping his back before pulling back. "Your mom said you'd be here tonight, eventually, but I wasn't sure I'd catch you."

Wyatt's stomach pinched. "I should've told you myself. Sorry."

"Don't apologize. You've had your hands full, and your mom said there's some sort of guardianship trouble. I don't want to make you talk about it twice, though, since you probably just went through it with your folks."

Wyatt winced. "Actually, I haven't been to the house yet."

"Ah. You wanted to see Beacon first."

"Guilty as charged." He'd been around horses all his life, since his parents bred quarter horses, but the chestnut gelding had long been his favorite. Before Wyatt left town he'd ridden Beacon daily if possible. Beacon was one more creature Wyatt had abandoned, but he wouldn't have taken the horse with him even if he'd had the space to keep him in Irvine. Wyatt hadn't been in any shape to give him what he deserved.

To give anyone what they deserved. That's why he left.

Something soft and damp nuzzled Wyatt's hand. The chocolate Lab gazed up at him with rich brown eyes. Wyatt reached down to pat the fellow, rubbing his silky ears while he replied to his cousin. "I know it doesn't say anything good about my character, visiting a horse before seeing my own parents, but I need a minute."

His emotions were too close to the surface right now, and his parents weren't much for discussing that sort of thing.

"You don't have to explain it to me." Mick's mom, sister to Wyatt's mom, had left him to be raised by Wyatt's parents, so he well understood the Teague preference to sweep unpleasant emotions and topics beneath a metaphorical rug. "Animals have a way of settling us down, don't they?" He made a pointed glance at the dog relishing Wyatt's strokes.

"Yeah, though it did me good to see you, too, cuz." He met Mick's gaze. "Who's this guy? Did you get a companion for Fly?" Fly was Mick's lone pet, but since Mick was a veterinarian, it wasn't unusual for him to bring home animal patients.

"No, this is Ranger. His owner passed a week ago and he needs a new home. The vet clinic is partnering with the animal shelter right before Valentine's Day to match up pets and people—My Furry Valentine. But until then, he's hanging out with me. As a retired therapy dog, he's accustomed to being with someone 24-7, so he's my helper right now."

It sure seemed like the dog was smiling at Wyatt, with his mouth open like that. "Service dog? Way to go, Ranger."

"He seems to like you."

"Maybe because I have baby food all over my shirt." With a final rub of the dog's neck, Wyatt stepped aside. "All right, pup, time for me to visit Beacon."

Mick gestured. "Actually, he's in the box on the right."

Wyatt recognized a roll of purple compression tape in Mick's hand, and he put two and two together. He rushed into the box and sure enough, there was Beacon, a chestnut gelding with a white blaze, his lower right foreleg wrapped in purple. "What happened?"

"Just a scrape from misstepping in mud. I just changed the bandage, and everything looks great." Mick followed him into the square, straw-lined stall.

"Is that true, Beak? You're better?" Wyatt stroked the gelding's blaze. "You've got the best vet in Goldenrod."

Beacon shifted closer to Wyatt, leaning into his touch.

Something flanked him from the other side, pressing against his knee. Ranger had planted himself beside Wyatt, clearly at ease with the horse.

"I'm getting sandwiched." Wyatt laughed.

"I think Ranger *really* likes you." Mick's serious tone drew Wyatt's gaze. "I mean it. Like he senses you might… I don't know. Need him."

"What kind of therapy dog was he, before he retired?"

"His owner suffered from trauma-induced anxiety."

"So, he's sensing anxiety right now? We Teagues never get anxious." The answer blurted out, born of habit. It was something his dad often said when they were growing up.

The past few months, however, he'd begun to wonder if his dad wasn't stating a fact—because who was never anxious?—but was instead reinforcing that anxiety wasn't normal. *God gave us emotions for a reason*, Alex always said. *They shouldn't rule us, but that doesn't mean they're a weakness we should ignore, either.*

Okay, I won't ignore it. The past few days had been difficult, and today was stressful. Anxiety was present. But technically, anxiety was not his main problem, and there was no way the dog could sense what was really wrong with him.

"Not anxiety, necessarily." Mick studied him. "Maybe

Ranger senses you could use a friend. And he's telling you he's available."

"Hold up. Are you asking me to take him?"

"I hadn't planned on it, but if you kept him for a few days, it would help me out. Tomorrow I'm heading out of town for training on new anesthesia equipment, and I would hate to leave him alone."

Wyatt scratched the back of his neck. "I guess I could. Temporarily. I'll either be sleeping here or at the McHughs', and there's room for him to run outside at both of those places." Hopefully, Natalie wouldn't mind.

"Thanks, Wyatt. I owe you."

"That's not how I see it. I—"

"Well, look who finally made it." A tall, burly man in his midfifties stood in the aisle, alongside a daintier woman of similar age with short brown curls. "Howdy hey, son."

"Dad. Mom." It had been so long since he had seen his parents that he lifted his mom off the ground, hugging her. Embracing his dad was more like hugging a tree. It was large, solid, and it didn't do much in the way of holding back.

But his dad was grinning when they broke apart, tapping his graying mustache as if deep in thought. "This stranger looks a lot like our son, doesn't he, Jillian?"

"I don't know, Gary," she joked. "It's been so long since he visited, I can't remember what he looks like."

Wyatt held up his hands in surrender. "Message received. I won't stay away this long again."

His dad entered the box and bent to examine Beacon's leg. "How's our boy here, Mick?"

"He'll be good as new in no time, Uncle Gary."

"Let's go back to the house." Wyatt's mom gave his dad a look. "I'll put on a pot of decaf, and you can fill us in on what happened today. Any decisions made about the twins?"

"It's complicated." His parents would want the facts, not how he felt about things. And they wouldn't pry. They never did. For the first time, he admitted to himself that it made him feel alone.

But as they left the stable, Wyatt remembered Jesus's promise never to forsake him. And, as Ranger trotted beside Wyatt, it felt like they were tethered by an invisible leash.

I'm not alone, am I? I've got You, God.

And apparently Ranger. Wyatt couldn't help but smile.

On Saturday evening, as the sun began its descent behind the trees, Natalie let herself out of the McHughs' kitchen door onto the patio as she rubbed the back of her neck. What a week, caring for Rose and Luna with Wyatt, which was…weird. No other word for it.

They had formed a partnership, of sorts. He handled the removal of the felled cedar tree and cottage demolition for her, which she appreciated, and she made him a pot of his favorite tomato soup. In their time together, they didn't discuss anything touchy, thankfully, sticking to safe topics like Foxtail and the weather.

And, of course, the babies.

And the senior dog that had showed up with Wyatt the morning after his return to town. Ranger's arrival might have been a surprise, but he wasn't an unwelcome one. Natalie loved animals, and she understood that as a former therapy dog, Ranger wanted to be with people. It didn't hurt, either, that Ranger—like the babies—proved to be a distraction when they might otherwise have started talking about something difficult.

Like Forrest and Cady's passing. Or the fact that their

friends had no surviving parents or siblings, so they had chosen Wyatt and Natalie to raise their children. Or that Natalie and Wyatt felt so out of depth that they intended to talk to Forrest's cousin about taking the girls.

The particular talk? Now or never. Natalie prayed for strength, tired as she was after such a long day, first with Cady and Forrest's joint funeral, and now the reception at their house, which she and Wyatt hosted. Pockets of guests lingered in the main rooms, but there were still two people neither she nor Wyatt had been able to speak to. Wyatt was changing a diaper, and while she could wait for him, she didn't want to miss this opportunity.

"Hendrick, Gwyneth." She strode over to the couple seated on Adirondack chairs, staring out at the mountain view. The temperatures were in the low forties, cool enough to send a shiver over Natalie's skin, but Hendrick and Gwyneth didn't seem bothered by the cold. "If you have a moment, I wanted to talk to you about Forrest and Cady's estate."

"Excellent timing, Mattie." Gwyneth tipped her head, inviting Natalie to take a seat. "Can you recommend a local Realtor who can sell this house for us?"

"It's Natalie. And the house, along with the rest of the estate, is actually in a trust for the twins. Wyatt is executor."

"Oh, that makes sense, to provide for the girls. We just assumed since I'm pretty much Forrest's only relative, his house would go to me. Not that I want it." Hendrick's voice held a faint tinge of condescension. "It would be such a bother to handle the sale while we're on the French Riviera, you see, but now we don't have to worry about it, Nicki."

"My name is Natalie. You're leaving the country again? You were just on vacation."

"That was play, but this is for work. As a travel writer,

I'm constantly on the go." Hendrick's eyes narrowed. "But wasn't there something you wanted to talk about? You mentioned the estate, but if it doesn't have to do with the house, then what is it?"

Natalie took a deep breath. "The girls, actually."

"They are so cute." Gwyneth's blue eyes rolled as if she were savoring dessert. "I love that they have flower names. Rose and—is it Violet? Iris?"

"Luna. It's not a flower that I know of." Natalie's heart pounded. "The thing is, Forrest and Cady named Wyatt and me as guardians but listed you as alternates if we are unable."

"Us?" Gwyneth laughed. "Thank goodness it hasn't come to that."

Hendrick frowned. "Now, Gwynnie, we'd do our part if we had to."

"Of course. Sorry, I don't hate children, honest." She toyed with her silver bracelet. "But can you imagine? We're on the road more than half the year."

Hendrick shrugged. "The staff would help while we're gone, of course."

Gwyneth snapped her thin fingers. "If we did take them on, I'd call Mira to decorate the nursery. White on white. It's so chic right now," she told Natalie. "Mira's the hottest interior designer in the state. Would you like her contact information? She travels to us from San Francisco whenever we need a refresh, so I'm sure she'd come here and polish up your place."

"Not right now, thanks." Natalie realized she was clutching the arms of the Adirondack. This conversation hadn't gone at all how she had expected.

A shrill cry carried from the house. Natalie was still learning to differentiate the girls' cries, but this sounded like Luna's hungry cry. Natalie stood. She was formulating how to ask if they could speak later, with the lawyer if necessary, when Gwyneth burst into laughter.

"The lungs on that kid! Good thing we weren't Forrest's first choice to adopt them or whatever."

"Constant headaches from the noise," Hendrick agreed. "Sounds like it's time for us to leave, Gwynnie."

Natalie went back inside, finding Wyatt in the kitchen, Ranger by his side and a fussy Luna in one arm while he set a container of pureed sweet potatoes on the counter. Glancing up, he gave an apologetic smile. "Rose is okay, but Luna's getting hungry."

"She's probably overwhelmed, too." Natalie reached into the cupboard for two baby bowls. "It's been a long day for the babies."

"For all of us. Lots of tears and heartache, but the number of people at the funeral and here at the house demonstrated how much Forrest and Cady meant to the community."

"There were so many people. I'm not sure I was able to greet everyone."

"Which reminds me. About twenty minutes ago, Sadie got hit with one of her migraines. With so many people in the house, she couldn't find you, so she told me to tell you sorry for leaving, and she probably won't see you tomorrow."

"Poor Sadie." Her sister's occasional migraines were the only thing, other than illness, that kept her from church. "I'll text her later, but hopefully she'll be sound asleep."

Wyatt snapped Luna into the high chair. "Before more people leave, maybe we should ask someone to feed the girls for us so we can find Hendrick and Gwyneth. It's essential we talk to them."

"They just left, but the three of us had a brief chat first."

She glanced at Luna, measuring her words. "Let's not discuss it in front of the girls, though."

Wyatt nodded. "Sure."

Once people realized it was the babies' mealtime, the guests cleared, leaving Natalie and Wyatt to feed the twins while they picked at leftovers from a deli tray Natalie's sisters had provided for the reception. Once the girls were bathed, given bottles, and settled in their cribs, Natalie and Wyatt retreated to the living room, where Ranger had found a comfortable spot for a snooze on the hearthside rug.

A low fire still crackled in the grate, its orange and blue flames defying the gloom like a symbol of hope amid their grief. Wyatt reached for the fireplace poker and coaxed a smoldering log. "It's your night to stay with the girls, but I'm happy to trade off so you can get a solid night's sleep."

"Thanks, but I want to be close to the girls right now." She switched on the baby monitor set atop the coffee table and kicked off her kitten heels, relishing the feeling of relief flooding her toes. "Plus, it will be easier to take them with me to church in the morning—I started attending with Sadie shortly after you left town. She'll probably stay home and watch the livestream tomorrow, though, due to her migraine." Her middle sister and his cousin Mick were the only two committed Christian members of their families.

His wide grin surprised her. "I have a relationship with God now, too. I had planned to go to church tomorrow, but I can't sit with Mick since he's playing guitar during the service. May I go with you and the girls?"

All four of them? Like a family? Mom, Dad and two babies in the pew, bumping shoulders and sharing a bulletin? Glad as she was that he was on speaking terms with the Lord now, her heart sputtered. "I don't know if that's—"

A loud, panicked screech pierced the stillness, and a red

light flashed on the baby cam. On the monitor's screen, Natalie could see Rose pulling up to stand in her crib, her tiny face contorted with anguish.

Natalie was up the stairs before she could think, scooping the wailing baby from her crib. "Rose, sweetheart? What is it?"

She didn't know Wyatt—and Ranger—were in the room, too, until Wyatt leaned over Luna's resting form. "I think she'll go back to sleep. Take Rose out and I'll be there once I settle Luna down."

Natalie clutched Rose to her chest and hurried downstairs, eager to examine her in brighter light. Back in the living room, she laid Rose on the couch and checked the screaming baby from head to toe.

Wyatt and Ranger appeared after a minute. "Luna's okay. Any idea what's going on?" He knelt by the couch to cup Rose's head, which was bright red from crying.

"It's not her diaper, her clothes aren't pinching her, and there's no rash or fever. I don't think she's hungry, because she just had a bottle. Maybe a nightmare, but she seems in so much pain." Natalie gulped in a large breath. "I should call the pediatrician. No, it's after hours. Let's go to the emergency room, unless you think we should call 911?"

"Before we do that, take a breath. It's tempting to panic—"

"She's in pain, Wyatt. Of course I'm panicking." Didn't he get it?

"Let me take her." His calm voice was a sharp contrast to Rose's anguished cries. With Ranger practically pressing into one of his legs, Wyatt held the baby upright against his chest and bounced gently.

"That's not fixing anything, Wyatt." Natalie was crawling out of her skin. *Lord, what do we do for this poor baby? She's suffering so.*

Wyatt's eyes narrowed. "I can feel her tummy against my chest. It seems fuller than usual." He rubbed large circles over her back, appearing to press harder than Natalie would have done. Then the cries cut off to give way to a loud burp, accompanied by a spurt of curdled milk that coated Wyatt's shoulder.

Rose blinked, then resumed crying, but this time like a tired baby, not an agonized one.

Natalie reached for her, but Wyatt shook his head. "Let me try a little longer in case she has anything more to come up. My shirt's already in need of the washer's heavy-duty cycle."

His light attempt at humor had its desired effect, and she felt a small smile tug at her mouth. "I'll get a cloth to clean you both up."

She returned from the kitchen with two damp washrags. Thankfully, Rose had stopped crying and was snuggled against Wyatt's shoulder—the one not soaked in milk. Gently, Natalie dabbed the baby's cheeks and chin with one warm rag, and then handed the other to Wyatt. "For your shirt."

"I wonder what caused her pain." Wyatt met her gaze over Rose's head. "Maybe the sweet potatoes don't agree with her?"

"Actually, I think it's my fault. I just remembered Cady saying Rose was such a fast eater that sometimes she swallows air and needs extra care after her bottle. Tonight things were so busy I don't think I burped her well enough before I laid her down in the crib. I'm so sorry."

Wyatt continued to rub gentle circles on Rose's tiny back. "All that matters is Rose is better now. We kept our heads and figured it out."

"*You* kept your head. I freaked out and almost called an ambulance."

"All right, then." His full lips quirked. "But you're the one who ultimately figured out the problem. We both played a part in getting here, Nat. It's teamwork. We always did balance each other out."

They did, didn't they? At the best of times, anyway. She gave structure to his life, and he added spark to hers. Memories of happy moments popped into her weary mind, but Natalie didn't want to dwell on them now. Too much had happened between them.

As little Rose burrowed her head on Wyatt's non-spit-up-on shoulder, he swayed and hummed softly. What was it about a man with a baby? It hit something deep within her. He couldn't fake the sort of care he was showing right now. Couldn't fake his heart.

He was a good man. He just hadn't loved Natalie as much as his job.

He did, however, care about these babies. And together, they had to make a difficult decision about what was best for them.

While Wyatt put Rose back to bed, Natalie sat in one of the wing-back chairs by the hearth. Rather than following Wyatt like he usually did, Ranger stayed with her, resting his chin on her leg. "Mick said you're an anxiety dog, huh? You must sense how hard this is for me. What are we going to do about the girls, boy?"

She prayed for guidance while she patted Ranger, but when Wyatt returned to the living room, she still had no answers.

"Rose is out cold." Wyatt cupped Natalie's shoulder. A comforting gesture that she wanted to lean into, but those days were over.

"Good." She bit her lip as Ranger shifted his attention to Wyatt.

Wyatt acknowledged Ranger's presence with a vigorous rub. "I know it's late, Nat, but we haven't yet talked about your conversation with Hendrick and Gwyneth. How did it go?"

She pulled a plush lap blanket over her legs to ward off the chill. "I presented the facts to them, but kids don't fit into their lifestyle. They were clearly relieved to hear they hadn't been Forrest and Cady's first choice as guardians. I'm sure the girls' needs would be met if they went to them, but I didn't feel they'd be loved as they deserve, so I didn't press the issue. It just won't work."

"I trust your instincts." Wyatt sat in the opposite chair. "But if they won't work as guardians, that leaves two choices, as far as I can see. Us…and foster care. And frankly, I don't even want to think about that second option."

"I don't either, Wyatt, but just now, what happened with Rose?" This part was almost too hard to speak aloud, but she met his gaze. "I think we have to ask ourselves, honestly, would Rose and Luna be better off away from us? Away from a former couple who can't get along and don't live in the same town, and placed with people who know what they're doing when it comes to taking care of children? Maybe Forrest and Cady made a mistake when they chose us."

Wyatt wondered the same thing about their friends' decision to name them as guardians without telling them. Wondered what on earth had been going through Forrest and Cady's minds.

"I wish we could ask them why they went about it the

way they did, but my guess is, Forrest and Cady chose us for a reason. Because they knew us. Or they chose us despite knowing us—"

He broke off. Forrest and Cady *knew* Wyatt.

Knew everything.

Including the secret Wyatt had been keeping for over nine months.

Yet Forrest and Cady hadn't changed their will in response to that knowledge.

It could've been an oversight, sure. But Wyatt wouldn't have put it past them to leave the will as it was on purpose. Because they knew Wyatt. Trusted him.

Believed he was more than his mistakes.

Wyatt met Natalie's gaze squarely. "I'm in awe of foster parents and the hard work they do, so don't get me wrong." He touched the edge of her chair. "But Rose and Luna shouldn't have to go into the foster care system. Not when they have us."

"There is no 'us.'"

"I didn't mean 'us' as a couple, Nat. I meant we are two grown adults who care about them enough to set our differences aside to bring them up together."

"We've been through this, though. You don't live in Goldenrod. Are you quitting your job?"

He couldn't do that. His work designing prefabricated homes was satisfying, and he was good at it, just as he was when he occasionally helped with construction. But there was nothing like it in Goldenrod for him. That was the main reason why he left town nine months ago. "You know as well as I do that I won't find comparable work here. The only architecture firm left in town is Crown, and they don't hire anyone outside their family."

"I hope you're not suggesting that I move to Irvine so

we're in the same place, because remember, I can't. Dad's will says I have to live at Foxtail for four more years or Dove and Sadie and Thatcher lose everything."

"I would never ask you to leave Foxtail." Which left them in a lurch. Except—

"It dawns on me that I'm entitled to eight weeks of family leave."

"Eight weeks?" Natalie's jaw dropped. "That's…a lot. You didn't think of it until now?"

"It's normally something people at the office do when they have a new baby. That's not exactly our situation. But two months off work would enable the girls and I to get to know each other better. Help them ease into the transition of our custody arrangement."

"What will that arrangement look like, anyway? Splitting custody like a lot of divorced parents—I have them during the week, and you can come visit them here on weekends?"

He hated how that idea felt in his gut. "I don't know. Maybe the next two months will give us time to figure things out. Let's just focus on spending time with the girls for now. Tomorrow I'll reach out to Solomon about my leave." His boss. "This is overwhelming, but we'll work things out, I promise."

"You didn't honor your promise to me nine months ago," she blurted. "You left."

There it was, the core of it all between them.

"It was more complicated than that, but yes. You asked me to choose between my job and you, and I chose to go." It felt like his chest was about to crack into two.

"How can we raise children together, Wyatt? Whether we live in the same town or not, I can't see it working. We were a team once, maybe, but we *broke*." Her voice trembled on the word. "And if things get difficult and you disappear after the girls bond to you, you'll break them, too."

Was this really about the girls, or Natalie's experience of her father? When she was young, her dad had abandoned his family and then come back to reunite with her mom, what, five times, only to leave after a few weeks each time? It wasn't hard to understand Natalie's fears that he would leave her, and the girls, in the lurch.

"I'm not your dad. Nor am I the same person I was nine months ago. A year ago. Ten years ago, when we first met. Things might not have worked out between us, but I am committed to Rose and Luna, and I will not abandon them."

Color flooded her cheeks. "I can't believe I'm saying this, but okay. Eight weeks for the girls to get to know you and for us to figure out a plan for the judge, because if we don't step up, the girls will go elsewhere. And even though I'm the one who mentioned foster care, it's not what I want, either. I just want the girls to be okay."

"I know. We both want what's best for them, but I think we can do this."

Even though it would mean years of biting his tongue when her control issues went on overdrive. A lifetime of his heart feeling like an open wound around her.

And a daily—no, hourly—need for God's strength to be the man Natalie and the girls needed. To never give in to his secret addiction, which began last year when a doctor prescribed opioids for a back injury he sustained on a construction site.

Wyatt had admitted his problem to himself, taking advantage of the opportunity to move out of the county with his job—temporarily—so he could seek treatment without anyone in Goldenrod knowing. He had planned to come back when he had a solution to his job moving out of town, and a firm control of his addiction. Come back to Nat.

She deserved a whole man, not a shattered one.

But in his attempt to protect her, he'd hurt her.

He never wanted her to know he was an addict, and hopefully, she never would. He never thought it would be a problem, since she broke their engagement.

But because of the babies, they were bound together again.

Forever, like it or not.

Chapter Four

A rat-a-tat-tat knock at Cady and Forrest's front door the next morning alerted Natalie to Wyatt's arrival. She wasn't quite ready for church, but at least she was already dressed. She cast a quick glance at her reflection in the guest room mirror.

Not bad, considering how little time she'd had to prepare for the day. A swipe of concealer beneath her eyes hid evidence of her fatigue, and the loose bun at her nape disguised the fact that she hadn't had time to wash and blow-dry her hair this morning. She was grateful for her foresight in packing an easy outfit for this morning so she didn't have to waste time thinking about her wardrobe. A charcoal sweaterdress over black leggings was a basic staple for her—comfortable in the cold weather, and as an added bonus around the babies, the marled color hid a multitude of stains.

Except, apparently, for baby formula, which she could see now that she twisted away from the mirror. A thick trail of spit-up shone over her left shoulder like glaze on a doughnut. "Great."

The mess would have to wait. She rushed downstairs, through the living room, where the babies lay side by side on a thick quilt beneath a gym toy, and unlocked the door to admit Wyatt, along with a whoosh of frigid morning air tinged with a trace of his cedary aftershave. She had to admit, he looked even better than he smelled, wearing a dark wool jacket over a cream sweater. She recognized the cream-and-black plaid scarf hanging loosely around his neck as one she had given him two years ago, right after they became engaged.

It goes with everything and will keep your handsome neck warm, she had said when he opened the gift. Then she had wrapped it around his throat and gently tugged him down for a kiss.

She forced that sweet memory to the curb. Her current relationship with Wyatt was strictly business.

Well, that wasn't the correct word. They were the best options to raise two precious girls. And to do that, she needed to make every effort to be friendly.

She glanced down and noted the lack of dog. "No Ranger today?"

"Since he's not an actual therapy dog anymore, I thought maybe he should stay with Mom and Dad for the morning." They weren't churchgoers. Then Wyatt's gaze fixed on her messy shoulder. "Rose again?"

She nodded as she shut the door. "Note to self, the burp cloth doesn't work if it's not in the correct place. The material of my dress is so thick, I didn't even feel it. Anyway, aside from that lesson, I've learned I need to bring more changes of clothes next time I stay over." She and Wyatt would switch off tonight, so he would sleep at the house with the girls.

Wyatt followed her into the living room. Upon seeing him, the babies squealed and kicked.

He dropped to the floor to join them. "Good morning, Lu-lu and Rosie—wait, Nat." His tone changed from coochie-coo to all business in an instant. "Are you saying you don't have anything clean to change into? Maybe you can wear something of Cady's. Seems like you two were the same size."

Pretty much, but Natalie shook her head. "I can't bear to look in her closet. Not yet."

His nod was curt, as if he too were hesitant to dive into emotional territory. "Why don't you head over to your place for a fresh dress, then."

"It's okay. I'll just keep my coat on. There's too much to do here if we're going to make it to church by the opening hymn."

"Tell me what to do and I'll do it."

Did he not notice the babies still wore footie pajamas, not day clothes? Natalie almost sighed, but then she gritted her teeth. She had developed a habit of being angry at Wyatt, judging his motivations and actions. She couldn't do that if they were going to raise the girls together.

Besides, last night, she'd been the clueless one and he'd figured out how to help Rose. *We're both learning, Lord. Help me to be patient with him as I want others to be patient with me.*

"The girls are still in their pajamas and their diaper bag needs to be refilled." She hoped she sounded as kind as she wished.

"I'll take the girls, you pack the bag."

"Deal." She bustled to the kitchen and packed two clean bottles and formula, pausing by the kitchen sink to dab at the whitish blotch on her dress. The dress would require a thorough washing later, but at least for now, she wasn't in danger of smelling like yogurt someone forgot to put in the fridge. Then she hurried back to the living room, where Wyatt held a girl in each arm.

The babies were dressed to the nines, from the soles of their black patent leather shoes to their poufy, slightly too-big pink dresses to the enormous bow headbands atop their fuzzy heads.

"Don't they look awesome?" Wyatt gave them a little bounce. His shy smile gave away the fact that he was rather proud of himself.

Her breath hitched. "They're, um…they're adorable."

His smile melted. "Are you worried they won't be warm enough? Or you don't like what I chose?"

"No, they have coats. You did great. It's just that those are their Easter outfits."

"Oh, okay. I guess that means we need to save them a few more months. I'll switch them into something else." He stepped toward the staircase.

She held him back with a hand on his arm. "That's not what I meant. I was thinking how Cady was so excited to buy those dresses, but now, she and Forrest won't be here for the girls' first Easter. Or any holiday, here on out."

Don't cry. You'll upset the babies and you don't have time to waste, remember? She blinked away tears and forced a smile worthy of how cute the babies were in their dresses. "The girls look precious, and I think they know it." Luna had a fistful of her pink tulle skirt heading toward her mouth, and Rose beamed as she reached for Natalie. Taking the little girl from him, she moved toward the pile of coats on the chair by the door. "Let's get these on."

"First, will that work with your dress?" The jut of his chin directed her gaze toward a thin rectangle of folded black and cream plaid wool, neatly laid on the coffee table.

The scarf he wore this morning.

Wyatt reached around her and picked it up by an edge, unfurling it. "I thought it might cover Rose's spit-up if you want to take your coat off. It's probably not your fashion choice."

She started to refuse out of habit, but she had agreed to get along with him for the girls' sakes, hadn't she? And there was honestly no good reason not to. "It's perfect. Thank you."

Wyatt, still holding Luna, stepped close enough to Natalie to wrap the scarf around her neck. The scents of cedar and musk clinging to him unleashed a flood of memories and emotion. Despite herself, she inhaled fully, lost in the past for a moment.

Willing herself back to the complicated present, she wound the scarf around her neck, twisting and draping it so it covered her shoulder and back.

Wyatt looked up from fastening Luna's coat around her tummy. "I never understood how you do that."

"Do what? Tie a scarf?"

"Take something and make it into a prettier version of itself."

The way he watched her, admiringly, even, floored her. It took her a hot second to breathe again. *He's trying hard to be nice. We're putting aside our differences, aren't we?* But his comment nevertheless made her recall how he used to make her feel gooey inside.

"I watched a YouTube video," she said once she got control of herself. "Let's get these girls into the car."

Since the seats were anchored into Natalie's silver SUV, they took the girls to her car. Wyatt, on the driver's side, caught her gaze. "Want me to drive? I have something to show you on the way to church."

"Can it wait until after church?"

"It can wait until you're ready." He pulled from his coat pocket a small spiral-bound notebook, a smaller version of the sketchbooks he always used for jotting down architectural ideas when they were dating.

Curiosity pricked at her. "Sure." She tossed him her keys. It wasn't like he had never driven this car. "Is it something for your job?"

"Nope." He got behind the wheel and started the ignition. "It's for you."

"Me?" She buckled into the passenger seat and shivered as cold air blasted from the vents. Soon enough the car would be toasty warm, but now it felt like an icebox. Her fingers fumbled, opening the book.

"To replace the cottage. What do you think of something like this?"

The schematic sketches inside made her gasp. "A log cabin?"

Although the name didn't do justice to his sketches. They were far more luxurious-looking than *Little House on the Prairie*.

He grinned as he turned the car onto the main road. "The style fits with the mountain surroundings, and my design has more square footage than the previous cottage without all the wasted space, so the footprint is smaller. A loft, vaulted ceiling and high-end finishes for the guests."

She could easily imagine the stunning mountain view through the wall of windows at the back of the dwelling. "Everything looks pretty and practical. I love the porch— I can just see guests sitting on rockers, enjoying the evenings." She looked up at him. "It's lovely, and you're right, it's more in keeping with the Cuyamacas than the New England–style cottage was. Maybe someday I can investigate doing something like this."

"Not *someday*. If you like it, we can do it now, and it

can be finished in time for that wedding so you don't have to cancel the reservation."

Natalie shut the book. "Be serious."

"I am."

"Then be realistic. Dating you taught me a few things about the construction process. The permit phase alone can take months."

"Not if it uses a prefabricated design I drew up for my firm, tweaked so it looks like a cabin, and we do it as a park model," he clarified. "I suggest pouring a concrete foundation and— Well, we can talk details later."

"You truly believe this could be accomplished in under three months? Utilities and everything?"

"I worked in Goldenrod most of my career, so I know the regulations well. The permits won't be a problem, and I know which contractors to hire. Another thing to keep in the back of your mind is the possibility of erecting two more cabins in the future. Tiny house size, but still. Triple the bookings eventually." At a stop sign, he met her gaze. "I can do this. I've got plenty of time, being on family leave."

That brought her back to earth. "I thought you were using your time off work to take care of the babies with me. Watch them while I work. They're a full-time job, you know."

"Oh, I know. But I'm willing to do everything I can to care for the girls and build that cabin before that wedding. It's just a matter of scheduling. I can work on it when the girls sleep." He scrutinized her dubious expression. "Why not, Nat? What do you have to lose?"

She stared at him as he parked in the church lot. "Why are you doing this?"

"Because you—Foxtail—need this, and it is something I'm very, very good at."

True, but there had to be more behind his motivation. Guilt, maybe? Last night, he had promised he wouldn't leave the girls…a promise he hadn't kept when he'd made it to Natalie. Was he giving her this gift since he couldn't offer her his love?

An impatient squawk sounded from the back seat. Rose.

"A-ba-ba-ba," Luna chimed in.

"They're fine when the car is in motion, but once it's stopped, they lose all patience." Natalie unbuckled her seat belt. "They're ready to get out."

"What do you think, though?" Wyatt waggled the sketchbook.

"Are you certain it's doable? Not pie-in-the-sky dreaming, but a realistic timetable?"

"Why can't it be both, Natalie?" He grinned like a boy with a new toy. "It's realistic, but if you want changes to the design, I need to know now so we can start as soon as possible. You could talk to the insurance company tomorrow, even. Get the ball rolling." He quoted her an estimated cost, which was well within the amount her insurance company mentioned.

She wanted to say no, not because she didn't like the idea. Not even because she feared it wouldn't be ready in time. But because it was Wyatt. *Is that fair of me, Lord?*

Much as she didn't want her life any more intertwined with Wyatt's than it already was, his expertise and connections in building the cabin would ensure Foxtail could host that wedding and provide more income down the line. The cabin would be a blessing that could make a difference in Foxtail Farm's future.

She just didn't trust him…but her lack of faith had nothing to do with his abilities. He was excellent at his job.

"No, I like it how it is," she said at last. "Thank you."

The babies squawked again. "That's our cue." Natalie opened her car door.

"Hey! You made it!" Beatie and Dutch approached the car. "Just in time."

Wyatt grabbed the diaper bag and hoisted Luna into his arms. Natalie scooped up Rose as Dutch and Beatie waited. Chatting, they all made their way through the church's double red doors into the sanctuary, warm from the heating system and gathered parishioners. Before they could take two steps, a fortyish man with dark, wavy locks reached out to give Natalie a side hug.

"Good morning, Pastor Luke."

Wyatt shook the pastor's hand. "Thanks again for officiating the funeral yesterday. What a tribute to Forrest and Cady."

"I was honored, but there's one thing I neglected to do that I would love to remedy now, if you don't mind keeping the babies in the service with you for a few minutes before taking them to the nursery."

"I had planned to keep them with us, actually." Natalie didn't want the girls to experience any emotional distress, no matter how short-lived. They'd been through too much this past week.

"Perfect." Pastor Luke rubbed his hands together. "I'd like to bring the four of you up front and pray for you. It's a difficult time of loss and transition, and I can't imagine how challenging it's been to find yourselves guardians of these two little ones. Is that all right with you?"

"More than all right," Natalie said. "Wyatt?"

"Sure, I'm grateful for all the prayer we can get."

The pastor grinned. "See you up there in a few minutes, then. Now if you'll excuse me, I need to start the service."

Natalie reached for Wyatt's sleeve as they followed

Dutch and Beatie through the foyer. "How did he know we're going to take on co-guardianship? We've hardly told anyone about our plan to talk to Hendrick and Gwyneth. We only chose to do this together last night."

"Did you tell your sisters?"

"I texted them late last night, yes, but Sadie had a migraine, so she wouldn't have told anyone here, and Dove doesn't go to church."

"My guess is people assumed that you and I were taking on co-guardianship from the start. A lot of people know I'm in town and we switch off nights taking care of the girls."

Probably true, but before she could answer, Beatie waved at a young man in jeans and a flannel jacket seated toward the back of the church, his dark eyes wide and apprehensive. "There's Silas." She turned to beckon Natalie and Wyatt. "I'm so glad he finally came. Let's sit with him."

Natalie had wanted to sit in the back, anyway, in case the girls fussed during church. They settled into the pew, and Wyatt extended his hand to Silas. "Wyatt Teague."

"Silas Moore."

"Our right hand in the orchard," Dutch explained.

Natalie smiled at Silas. She didn't know the quiet man well, but he was a hard worker and had expert knowledge about trees and irrigation, according to Dutch.

The strains of the opening hymn began, and Natalie turned her attention to the service. It wasn't easy to concentrate, knowing they'd be going up to the front of the sanctuary in moments, but she was grateful for the opportunity to receive prayer.

Right before the sermon, Pastor Luke beckoned them forward. Natalie's heart warmed. She carried Rose while Wyatt carried Luna up to the front where the smiling pastor had them turn to face the congregation.

"Wyatt and Natalie need our support," Pastor Luke said. "And they'll need prayers as all four of them adjust to a new way of living. Let us pray."

Natalie bowed her head and closed her eyes, but a gentle touch on her shoulder—too big to be Rose's little hand—drew her to look up. Dutch had come alongside her to pray, and Beatie and Mick stood beside Wyatt. Members of her women's Bible study joined them to pray, too.

She felt humbled. Supported.

And like a complete fraud.

As much as she yearned for their prayers, was she worthy of them? These people were praying for her and Wyatt as if they were a team. A family.

She and Wyatt were nothing of the sort. Would their fellow church members pray with such zeal if they knew she'd broached giving up co-guardianship? Or if they had an inkling she feared he might leave her and the girls, sooner or later, so it was better not to partner with him at all?

Her skin crawled. But then Rose shifted, grasping a handful of Wyatt's scarf from Natalie's shoulder and pulling it to her mouth, reminding Natalie what was most important right now.

The girls.

She relaxed into the embrace of her spiritual family and joined in their prayers. Natalie had to try to work with Wyatt for the babies' sakes, and therefore, she and Wyatt needed all the prayers they could get.

It was chilly on Tuesday morning when Wyatt took Ranger and left his parents' house before the sun's first rays crept over the mountains. He wasn't due at Forrest and Cady's until eight, so he had just enough time to drive the few miles down the mountain to attend a six thirty recovery meeting at the downtown rec center first.

After the meeting, Wyatt whistled along to the country station on the radio as he drove the few blocks from the rec center to Forrest and Cady's house, Ranger by his side. The Lab had been a hit at the meeting, as if each person in attendance felt the dog's unconditional acceptance. It sure seemed as if everyone left with a smile.

Wyatt certainly did. He always felt better after meetings, grateful for the strength God provided in different ways. It helped to be with others, old and young alike, who were trying to stay free of addictive substances.

Wyatt had recognized one of members there as Silas, the Foxtail employee who had been at church on Sunday. Other than a brief nod of acknowledgment, Wyatt left Silas alone. The right to privacy was a core value in these meetings, for which Wyatt was grateful, because his own addiction was secret. Something he never wanted his family or friends to know.

And the stakes had gone up when he thought about permanently raising Rose and Luna. He was clean, sober and determined to stay that way permanently, with God's help.

But he couldn't help wondering: If Natalie knew about his past opioid addiction, would she try to keep the kids away from him?

All I ever wanted was to protect her, Lord. Now I want to protect the girls, too.

The best way he could see to do it was to ensure he stayed on the right path, and Natalie would never need to know how badly he'd failed.

After knocking, Wyatt let himself inside with his key. The house was toasty warm, and Ranger trotted straight toward one of the floor heating vents, curling up alongside it.

"We're in the kitchen," Natalie called.

He found the babies in their high chairs, Natalie spooning thin cereal into their mouths. "Am I late? Sorry." He shed his coat and moved to the sink to wash his hands.

"You're right on time." Natalie glanced at the clock on the kitchen wall, right under the country-style sign spelling out a Bible verse in cursive letters. *The joy of the Lord is your strength.*

A good reminder. Wyatt doubled down on claiming God's promise of strength as he pulled a chair around to take over feeding one of the girls. Actually, he could feed both of them. "You can go home, if you want. You must have a lot to do."

"I can work from here this morning, since I have several phone calls to make." She glanced up from spooning cereal into Luna's wide mouth. "Are the papers for the cabin ready to submit?"

"I finished preparing them last night." Yesterday, once Natalie's sisters and Thatcher approved the cabin designs and Wyatt spoke to his friend Alex about his ideas for a few tweaks, he had started work. Any talk of how he and Natalie would organize custody of the girls had been pushed to the back burner by unspoken agreement. The top priority was getting the cabin process off the ground now, because every day counted. "I'll give the documents a final once-over while the girls are occupied. I don't want to miss anything in the paperwork that could cost us time."

"I doubt that would happen. You're good at your job, Wyatt."

Was she actually complimenting him? Wyatt bit back a smile. "You are, too, Nat. Foxtail is in capable hands."

"Hands that are tied by my dad's will. Running the orchard and ranch according to his directions for four more years doesn't allow us many ways to grow, but the new rental cabin might help. In the meantime, I'm trying everything I can. Did you know Mick has some event at the animal shelter on the Saturday before Valentine's Day?"

"Yeah, he mentioned it. My Fluffy Valentine."

"Furry," she corrected with a smile.

"Are you involved in the event?"

"Foxtail is donating cider, and I've asked Sadie to talk to Mick about adding vendors. I think it would draw in more visitors, and if all the merchants agree to donate a portion of their proceeds to the shelter, it's win-win. If Mick says yes, then Foxtail can sell baked goods and floral arrangements."

"Every penny counts, for both the shelter and Foxtail." Wyatt's phone buzzed, and he pulled it from his pocket. "Huh. Dad wants my help with something on the ranch. He knows I have the girls today, but it sounds like it won't take more than a few minutes. Would you mind if the girls and I took a little field trip?"

"I guess not." She glanced at his phone just as a second text came in.

Alex. It could wait. Wyatt swiped stray baby cereal off his blue flannel shirt. "I know you have phone calls to make, but would you like to come, too?"

She leveled him with a look. "I—haven't been there since, you know."

"I know. They'd be glad to see you, though, and you can take your laptop with you if you want to work while they watch the girls. Dad says there's minestrone for lunch in the Crock-Pot. A change of scenery wouldn't hurt, and you'd be more than welcome."

His parents loved her. Everyone had been Team Natalie after Wyatt up and left, even his mom and dad.

She chewed her lip. "It might be good to get out of the house."

"We can pop the girls in the stroller and take a walk. It's cold now, but the temperature is supposed to go up, and the girls might like to see the horses." He smiled at the girls. "Do you want to see the horsies?"

Rose's little hands batted the high chair tray, and Luna made a happy noise.

"See?" Wyatt grinned. "They want all four of us to go."

"I'm pretty sure they don't know what a horse is, Wyatt."

"That's a travesty that requires immediate attention."

She chuckled. "Okay. As long as I can make my work calls while we're there and we're back before the girls' afternoon nap. Do you mind getting them ready while I call the insurance company?"

"Not in the least." First, though, Wyatt read Alex's text.

Checking in. Praying for you. How are things with Natalie?

Was that code for *have you told her yet?* Wyatt stifled a groan.

Thanks for praying. Taking things day by day. Maybe we can catch up tonight once the girls are in bed.

Then, Wyatt texted his dad.

Nat is coming along. Please don't make it awkward.

An hour or so later, they pulled into Manzanita Ranch, named for the native trees that populated the land. *Little apple* in Spanish, but the only similarity between the trees that grew at Foxtail and the red-barked manzanita was the tiny, apple-like fruit that appeared each summer.

Wyatt's parents met them outside the house with hugs for Natalie and enthusiastic greetings for Rose and Luna.

"Do you remember me from Saturday, cuties? You do, don't you?" His dad took Luna from Natalie.

Wyatt's mom reached for Rose. "Gary, is this what it's like having grandchildren?"

"Mom." Wyatt grabbed the diaper bag and Ranger's leash out of the car.

"What? I raised four children, and not one of you has given us grandkids. Your sisters moved away and are in no hurry, and Mick says he's never getting married. Your dad and I aren't getting younger, you know."

He mouthed *Sorry* to Natalie.

She shrugged, then smiled at his mom. "You sound like my mother."

"How is Yvonne?" Mom carried Rose into the house, and the rest of them trailed behind. "We were sorry to miss her at the funeral."

"Her hip replacement prevented her from making the trip," Natalie said.

Although Wyatt suspected Yvonne probably wouldn't have come to the service, even if she hadn't been laid up. She lived in San Diego, an easy drive to Goldenrod, but she rarely visited Foxtail. Too many bad memories of her marriage to Asa, she said. But Wyatt felt sad that her bitterness seemed stronger than her desire to support her daughters.

"Thanks for coming so fast." Wyatt's dad led them into the living room, where his parents had set out infant toys. Had they gone shopping? "I noticed a swale in the roof of the old barn we use for storage. I could use an architect's opinion."

"It might be storm damage that we initially missed." His mom lowered Rose to the quilt beside a stack of baby books. "I'm happy to play with the babies if you need to work while Wyatt checks it out, Natalie."

"I'll take you up on that, Jillian. Thanks."

"You know where the office is."

The morning passed quickly. Unfortunately, the barn's roof was in worse condition than anticipated, so Wyatt assisted his dad in covering the supplies with sheets of plastic to protect them from any rain that might come before they could get a new roof. After a hearty lunch of minestrone and sourdough bread, they bundled the babies back up in their coats and caps, whistled to Ranger, and wandered to the south paddock to take a walk. Wyatt had built benches around one of the large oak trees, and it was a nice spot to sit and enjoy the green field and grazing horses.

Peaceful. Serene, with his parents each holding a baby and the gentle breeze rustling through the branches overhead. Until Wyatt's phone buzzed.

Natalie's peek at the screen wasn't as discreet as she probably thought it was. Was she curious or mistrustful? Probably both. He tipped the screen toward her. "It's Solomon."

"It must be important, for your boss to contact you while you're on family leave."

"He has questions about some projects." Wyatt sighed, tapping out a response.

"You're entitled to this time off." Natalie's disapproval was evident in her pinched lips.

"It's important to keep your boss happy so you don't lose your dream job." Dad looked at his watch. "Want to ride Beacon before you go? He could use a short walk after his injury."

"Injury?" Natalie's lips parted in surprise.

"A scrape. Nothing major, but he's been resting," Wyatt explained.

"Poor Beacon. You're his favorite, so you should be the one to ride him first after something like that."

"I don't want to leave you stranded."

"We're having a lovely time, and the girls won't be ready for their nap for a while. Go!" She shooed him away.

"I won't take long."

Ranger followed him to the stable. He hadn't saddled Beacon in three-quarters of a year, but muscle memory took over, and it wasn't long before he led the gelding into the yard and lifted his boot in the stirrup, pulling himself astride.

The smell of horse and the whisper of the wind filled his senses as they ventured slowly onto the flat riding trail. He'd forgotten how the reins felt in his fingers, how soothing the swaying movement could be. While he, Beacon and Ranger kept a slow, steady pace on the path, he marveled at the scents of damp earth and horse, the sounds of steady hooves and the dog's panting breaths, and the feel of the winter sunlight on his cheeks.

He felt like a version of himself he hadn't been in a long time. Stronger, more peaceful, not thinking about his job or his addiction or anything stressful.

How long had it been since he'd been able to live in the moment quite like this?

Not since the days before he hurt his back on a construction site and the doctor prescribed those strong painkillers. Since then, he'd put in hours of work to get healthy, but in leaving town to do it, he had cut himself off from several things he'd taken for granted.

Things that were a part of him. Like being in nature,

just a man and his horse…and, as Ranger trotted along-side, a dog.

And his loved ones. Even the woman he'd hurt.

Could they be part of his healing, too? Or would he mess up, as Natalie seemed to expect?

Wyatt wasn't like her father. But he had poked all those familiar wounds in Natalie when he left, causing her pain when he'd meant to avoid it. He saw that now.

All he could do was pray for Natalie, and a future that was best for her, Rose and Luna. Hopefully, Wyatt's addic-tion would stay secret, buried too deep to hurt any of them.

Chapter Five

"We need to talk about the April wedding in the orchard." Natalie tapped her pencil on the nicked oak conference table in the Foxtail Farm office.

She, her sisters and their cousin Thatcher were gathered for a staff meeting, polishing off a plate of Dove's apple muffins and a pot of coffee as they worked their way through Natalie's long agenda. They hadn't sat down to discuss Foxtail matters like this since the babies came to Natalie, almost three weeks ago. How could it already be the second Friday in February? "How are we with the bridal flowers, Sadie?"

"As fine as possible. It's too soon to have the flowers all figured out down to the last petal." Sadie reached for a second muffin.

Not according to the bride, Esme Holtz. "Esme texted me again this morning."

Dove threw her hands in the air. "Here we go. What do she and her lifestyle columnist mom want this time?"

Knowing that Esme's mom would indubitably write up an article on the wedding added pressure to get the celebration as perfect as possible, but Esme's continual requests were starting to get on everyone's nerves.

Natalie took a deep breath. "She's worried none of the

trees will be in bloom for the wedding. Since she specifically wants apple blossoms in the bouquets, Sadie—"

"I've got it covered." Sadie covered Natalie's hand with her own. "I assured her that the Cripps Pinks bloom earliest, so it should be fine, but if there are no blooms in the orchard on her wedding date, I can source some from outside Foxtail for her bouquet and hairpiece. I'm competent at my job," she tacked on with a laugh.

An understatement. Sadie was a creative florist, whose talents were largely limited since she was bound to Foxtail Farm. Bouquets and plants for sale at the farm stand, along with the occasional gig crafting custom orders, surely didn't satisfy her. But, like Dove, Thatcher and Natalie, she was making sacrifices to ensure they didn't lose the farm.

"She understands the orchards might not be blooming on her wedding day, right? Because we don't control the weather." Thatcher's droll tone told them how ridiculous he thought this was.

"She signed a contract saying so." Natalie had been sure to include it in the legal document. "And she's willing to get married in the orchard of whichever apple variety looks best at the time. But lately she's been texting a lot, sounding anxious and dissatisfied. At least the cabin changes met her approval."

"I'm starting to think Esme is a bridezilla. She emailed me changes to the cake's decorations and catering menu." Dove would bake the wedding cake but was also overseeing arrangements with Esme's caterer for the dinner reception at the orchard's edge after the ceremony. "She accidentally included a list to include with the wedding invitations. Female guests are forbidden from wearing pink so they 'aren't confused' with the bridesmaids. That's going too far, in my opinion."

Wow. Natalie jotted it down on her notepad. "I guess we'll all make a point of wearing black, to be on the safe side. With Foxtail lanyards, so everyone knows we're staff."

"If we're just going to talk wedding stuff, do I need to be here?" Thatcher scooched back in his chair. "The cattle and I have no involvement in that stuff whatsoever."

Dove shifted, as if she, too, were ready to end their meeting. "And it's not like I can bake the cake now, or Sadie can do the flower work. Why discuss it?"

"Because we all need to be up to speed." Natalie fought a wave of irritation. "This wedding will give us a financial boost. So far, this quarter has been dismal."

"Winter is always lean," Sadie noted.

"Always." Dove toyed with her coffee mug. "Tourists stop for pies, but it's not like there's any other reason for them to visit Foxtail at this time of year."

"Which is why we need more ways to bring in income beyond apples, farm stand goods and the little beef we sell." Didn't anyone understand how important this was? "I wish we could plant berries for summer U-picking. Or add a petting zoo, or better yet, extend the cattle ranch into some of the back acreage that's just sitting there doing nothing, and rent out the rest."

"But we can't, due to your dad's will. No additions to the property, no new crops, no renting out the undeveloped land or expanding boundaries, nothing that would help us out of the pickle we've been in since Uncle Asa died." Thatcher leaned back in his chair. "Just a few more years."

"One down," Dove said.

"Four to go," they all mumbled.

Sadie's phone buzzed, and she started to text. "Sorry. It's Mick. We're meeting up later."

"Ooh," Dove teased. "You two 'friends' finally dating already?"

Sadie rolled her eyes. "Does no one understand platonic friendship anymore? And for your information, Nosy Posy, we're working on final plans for My Furry Valentine."

The shelter event was the next topic on Natalie's agenda. "Are we ready to go for tomorrow?" Foxtail would sell Valentine bouquets and baked goods.

"Ready," Sadie said.

"Absolutely, but other than this event, I want to forget Valentine's is coming." Dove scribbled in her notebook. "All this mushy stuff makes me miss Gatlin. We won't even be able to FaceTime."

She hadn't seen her boyfriend since his Marines unit had deployed a few months ago.

"Then let's celebrate Galentine's Day," Sadie offered. "Sorry, Thatcher, you're not included."

"I'm relieved not to be invited to your rom-com–watching, toenail-polishing night."

"I thought we'd go out for Thai, then try that new axe-throwing place."

"I might be interested, then." Thatcher rubbed his chin.

Natalie sighed. "You can take my place. I'll be spending Galentine's with my little gals. Let's get back on track, though. Sadie, you'll be sure to have enough flowers for the farm stand, too, right? We did well with that Valentine table last year, but as I recall, we decided to go bigger this year."

"It's all arranged." Sadie's smile softened her words. "You don't need to micromanage everything."

It came out like a tease, but this was a sore spot. This wasn't the first time someone had accused Natalie of being a bit of a control freak. Well, someone had to make the tough calls, and it sure seemed like the buck always stopped at her desk. "I'm not sure you all understand how precarious our situation is. What if Foxtail fails?"

"It won't." Thatcher shrugged. "Simple as that."

The way her cousin moved caused a pang of recognition in her. "You sure look like Dad sometimes." Her lips twitched. "And act like him."

He adopted an expression of mock pain. "Hey, I'm not that big of a ladies' man."

"I meant the unwavering optimism in the face of doom," Natalie quipped. "No comment on the other part."

"Ouch." Thatcher's hand went to the placket of his blue plaid shirt.

Natalie's phone buzzed, a text from Wyatt with an accompanying photo. Dove spied it and patted the table with excitement. "Open it. It's the babies."

They'd never get through the meeting's agenda at this rate. Natalie tapped her phone screen. Sure enough, Wyatt had sent her a photo of the girls in their pink caps and coats in the double stroller, accompanied by a text.

Heading out to watch the foundation get poured.

Sadie bent over the table to peek at the photo. "They look so cute."

"Aww, Luna's holding the elephant I got her," Dove said with a grin.

"Why don't we join them? I wouldn't mind watching." Thatcher puffed out a breath, looking so much like Dad it hurt.

She both missed her father and wished she could sit him down and demand answers. *Why, after years of breaking promises to us kids, did you leave us the farm like this,*

Dad, with so many strings? You wanted us to work together, that's obvious.

Goodness, was that why Forrest and Cady hadn't changed their will? They'd wanted Wyatt and Natalie to work together for some ridiculous reason? Reconciliation? Romance?

Pah. Now that Natalie was caring full-time for the twins, she could see how easy it was to put off scheduling appointments. The babies were delightful, but they required round-the-clock effort that, when combined with her Foxtail tasks, left her exhausted by the end of every day. And Wyatt was working hard, too, between the girls, some tasks for his boss despite being on paid family leave, and ensuring the cabin was finished in time.

Dove's gentle nudge brought Natalie back to the present. "How are things with Wyatt?"

Sadie stared at her, and even Thatcher didn't seem as eager to bolt out of their meeting.

Natalie's face grew hot. "Fine. Cordial."

"That's it?" Dove seemed disappointed.

"Cordial is good." Thatcher nodded. "I don't want him getting any ideas."

"Do you have any closure with your relationship?" Sadie's voice was soft.

"We haven't talked about our breakup, if that's what you mean. We're keeping our focus on the girls and, frankly, just getting through each day. It's been so busy." Which was why Foxtail hadn't had a staff meeting in weeks. She started ticking off her fingers. "There have been meetings with the lawyer about Forrest and Cady's estate, held in trust for Rose and Luna. And hours spent on the cabin. Plans, permits, you know how it is."

"Those are thankfully done now, though." Sadie mimicked wiping sweat from her brow.

"Just in time for the girls to start crawling. We spent last night babyproofing, but this morning we learned we missed a few things."

"Like?" Thatcher's grin spread wide.

"Like I can't set my purse on a low table anymore or leave Ranger's food where they can get to it."

Thatcher and Sadie laughed, but Dove scowled. "Why am I just hearing they crawled, and why are there no photos of the twins grabbing kibble?"

"I was too busy grabbing the kibble before they could get to it to take a pic, Dove. And the crawling happened yesterday. Although, technically, Rose is the only one moving on hands and knees. Luna is doing an army-crawl sort of thing. Either way, they're mobile."

Sadie sat back. "Have you figured out the co-guardianship custody issues yet?"

Natalie's heart pounded in her ears. "No. I think I should keep the girls on weekdays, and he should come on weekends. That's when we're busiest at the farm, anyway. But he wants to split their care evenly."

"That sounds good." Sadie shrugged.

"Except he would need to be in town to do more with them, and that's not going to happen. He doesn't know yet how it's going to work, and it's hanging over me. I can't stand not knowing."

And he spends a lot of time texting someone named Alex. She didn't want to admit aloud how much it bothered her, especially when it was none of her business, but he never talked about it. Who was she? A girlfriend?

Ugh, this was going nowhere.

"You know what?" Natalie stood up from the table. "Let's go watch the concrete getting poured."

"Woo-hoo!" Thatcher hopped up and grabbed his Stetson from the hook by the door.

"Nat, I'm worried about your emotions in all of this." Sadie was persistent, that was for sure. "If you're going to be bound to your ex-fiancé for the next twenty years, don't you think you should talk about what went wrong?"

"There are more important things right now than sifting through our past. Like creating a routine with Rose and Luna and getting this cabin built." Natalie avoided making eye contact with her family as she slipped into her coat and walked out into the cloudy morning. Thankfully, they all took the hint and dropped the subject.

The rumbling sound of a cement-mixer truck grew louder as they rounded the trees to a busy construction scene. Wyatt, Ranger and the stroller stood well clear of the temporary orange fencing around a wooden formwork filled with rebar reinforcements. Now, concrete poured from the cement mixer into a smaller orange vehicle connected to a hose, held by a man wearing hip waders and boots. Was the noise frightening the girls? She hurried to the stroller, greeting Wyatt with a hasty nod.

She needn't have worried. Wyatt had thoughtfully placed earmuffs on both girls, who stared at the scene with rapt fascination. Rose, in fact, gripped the stroller's edge as if she might pull herself up and out—thankfully she wasn't old enough to do that yet. Luna's posture was more relaxed, as was typical for her personality, but her eyes were wide with curiosity.

Natalie's heart swelled inside her chest, grateful for the ability to engage with these little ones. Squatting beside the stroller, she pointed at the cement mixer. "See the drum in the big truck going round and round?"

Rose squealed, and Luna made a breathy sound.

Since they seemed to be enjoying themselves, Natalie made a mental note to look for a picture book about construction vehicles on their next visit to the library. They might only be nine months old, but their curious minds were absorbing so much about the world around them. Wyatt might enjoy reading a book like that to them, too, since it incorporated elements of his work.

Who would have thought a month ago that she would give a thought to looking for a baby book Wyatt would get a kick out of? She caught herself chuckling.

Wyatt bent beside her. "This is so cool, isn't it?" he asked in her ear.

A rhetorical question, because she had laughed, but the whisper of his breath sparked a shiver down her neck. She wished she hadn't responded that way, but how could she deny that Wyatt was attractive? They'd been engaged to be married, after all.

Still, it would be nice if that pull toward him had died with their romantic relationship.

He watched her, waiting for an answer, so she rose back to full height. "It is." Fun to watch—even more fun to watch the girls' interest—and a definite boon to her spirits to see evidence of the cabin's progress.

Wyatt had been right when he assured her things would move quickly once the permitting process was completed, thanks to his contacts and expertise. What would she have done without him in this process?

God, I never want to rely on Wyatt again. Yet here we are, and his help could save the farm. I should be glad, but... I don't want to be let down again. What am I supposed to do?

As the concrete topped the framework, the noise quieted, and Thatcher sighed. "I'd better get back to work."

"Same here." She bent to give attention to the girls. When she looked up again, Dove and Sadie had gone with Thatcher, leaving Natalie and Wyatt alone. Before she could speak, something wet hit her forehead. "Was that rain? It's not in the forecast."

"Yeah, the weather app on my phone is clearly wrong, because that's rain." Wyatt gestured at the crew, who were unfolding a tarp to cover the wet concrete.

"I hope we don't get much. I'd hate for attendance at My Furry Valentine to be low tomorrow."

"If it doesn't clear up, we can change the theme from Valentine's to Noah's Ark," he joked. "We can dress the girls in animal costumes. Bears. Or zebras."

"Why not dress up the shelter dogs, too?" She tapped her chin as if seriously considering the idea. "And us, of course. I'd be happy to find you a tunic and a long white beard to wear so you look like Noah."

"Sure, and you can dress up like the dove with the olive branch. Maybe Sadie can get us a big balloon arch that looks like a rainbow." His smile was so wide, his cheeks were round and rosy as crabapples.

"If only we could come up with such easy solutions to our real-life problems." She had meant it as a joke, but it was true.

"About that." His features grew serious. "I've been wracking my brains trying to come up with a way for me to share parenting duties while keeping my career, and I had an idea. I'm not saying it's a great idea, but I could ask my boss about remote work."

Natalie hadn't expected that. "Solomon hates the idea of remote work, doesn't he?"

"He would never go for it full time, you're right, but even a day or two a week would be better than nothing. And what if I sweetened the deal?" He tipped his head at the construction crew. "What if I propose cabin kits? If I spearhead something potentially lucrative, he might relent."

"It sounds like it has potential, but if Solomon says no, we're back to square one."

"Let's cross that bridge when we come to it." His smile was tight, but hopeful. "I'm praying for God to provide a solution, but rest assured, I won't let you or the girls down. I promise."

Promises, promises. She and Wyatt were different people than they were last year. But her heart was still bruised.

And she wasn't sure she could ever get over it.

"Thanks for helping me with this, guys."

The next morning, Mick reached into a cooler and offered glass bottles of cider pressed from Foxtail's apples to Wyatt and Thatcher. Last night's unexpected rain had stopped around midnight, and the morning was awash in pale winter sunlight. While there would be plenty of muddy paws at today's My Furry Valentine adoption event, at least the skies would be clear.

"Our pleasure, cuz. We want to find homes for all these animals, too." Wyatt quenched his thirst with a gulp of the sweet, icy cider. Hauling hay bales to create seating around the field was a piece of cake, but he had nevertheless worked up a sweat.

He, Mick and Thatcher took their break in the volunteer tent, set to the side of the animal shelter. Other volunteers, including Wyatt and Natalie's families and shelter staff, still bustled around with various tasks. The last time Wyatt had seen Natalie, she was tying heart-shaped balloons onto fence railings, but that job was completed. Ah, there she was, standing at a makeshift paddock, carrying Luna while Beatie held Rose, chatting with one of Goldenrod's eldest residents, Willard Thibodeaux. His business, Happy Hooves, brought gentle riding mares to kids' birthday parties and other events, and it was a perfect addition to the family-friendly atmosphere today.

Natalie looked so pretty with her dark hair trailing over her chunky red turtleneck sweater, smiling while she spoke to Willard and then the girls. Was she teaching the babies how to touch a horse gently? Describing the feel of its coat and mane to them? She was so good at this parenting thing, always guiding them, loving them.

When he came back to town a few weeks ago, he'd figured he would still be drawn to Natalie. How could he not, when he had loved her over half his life? He had fallen for her the summer he was fourteen, when they met at the rec center while she and her sisters spent their summer vacations with their dad. It took two more summers for him to gain the courage to ask her on a date. After that, they were peas in a pod. Living in different towns—Natalie in San Diego with her mom during the school year, and Wyatt here in Goldenrod—had no effect on their commitment to each other. When she graduated college and moved to Goldenrod permanently, they took their time before getting engaged, establishing their careers and dreaming of a bright future.

A future that would never come to be.

Yet he still cared for her. More than that. He felt like there was a magnet in his chest, pulling him toward her all the time, no matter the situation. Crying babies, sitting beside her in church—

"Speaking of finding homes." Thatcher's voice drew Wyatt back to the conversation. "Is Ranger up for adoption today?"

Wyatt didn't like that thought at all. "I forgot about that. Mick?"

"I think he found his forever home a while ago." Mick eyed Wyatt. "Don't you?"

He hadn't given conscious thought to Ranger's permanent home, but now that he did, he couldn't bear the thought of parting with him. "I do." Wyatt rubbed the dog's neck and ears, ruffling up the red bandanna Natalie had tied around his neck so he'd look "properly Valentiney."

Thatcher opened the doughnut box and grimaced. "Pink icing? Man, is everything going to be pink and red today?"

Wyatt gestured at the decorative streamers. "Dude, it's a Valentine's Day event."

Mick capped his drink. "My last shelter party didn't have a theme other than 'bring home a rescue,' but having a Valentine theme this time attracted more media attention."

Wyatt clapped his cousin's shoulder. "Looks like it's attracting customers, too." He pointed to the cars entering the makeshift parking lot. "Time to let the dogs out?"

"Hey, isn't that a song?" Thatcher laughed.

"Don't forget the thank-you lunch when this is over," Mick reminded them.

Wyatt took Ranger with him inside the shelter to collect an excited pit bull pup, and Ranger proved to be a calming influence while Wyatt led the younger dog to the areas marked off with temporary fencing and a sign reading Speed Dating, a tongue-in-cheek nod to the Valentine theme. There was plenty of help moving the animals outdoors, and within minutes he was free to join Natalie.

Willard had customers, and she had moved with the babies to stand beneath a banner that read Puppy Love. The babies sat forward in the stroller, watching the activity. When they saw him and Ranger coming, they grinned. Rose kicked happily, sending one of her shoes flying out in an arc.

Wyatt scooped up the pink slip-on and placed it back on her tiny foot. Then he cupped Luna's foot, too, so she wouldn't feel left out, and gave them both little shakes. "I saw you with the horsies. How were they?"

"Fun," Natalie answered for them. "I'm a little sad, though. Willard says he's ready to retire. No more Happy Hooves."

Wyatt couldn't remember a time without Happy Hooves in town. "What's Willard going to do?"

"Sell his land and move to the coast to be near his daughter." She sighed. "It's the end of an era."

"The end of one thing is always the beginning of another, though." Like their newfound, tentative friendship. One he didn't want to disturb by getting too heavy right now. "Since you don't need to work the Foxtail booth for a half hour or so, would you like to get a coffee? Or look at the vendor booths?"

"Both."

He pushed the stroller, and she held Ranger's leash. They stopped by the coffee booth for hot drinks and a pup cup for Ranger, and then took their time through the vendor area, pausing to look at homemade candles, knitted goods and soup mixes. While Natalie completed a purchase, Wyatt looked ahead to a booth overflowing with hair bows. One caught his eye. "Let's stop there next."

Tucking her prepackaged pea soup mix into the stroller's storage basket, she followed his gaze. Then she looked him up and down, from the collar of his flannel jacket all the way to his muddy work boots. "Hair bows? Who are you and what have you done with Wyatt Teague?"

It was almost like old times, with Natalie teasing him like that.

He adopted a look of mock pain. "What's wrong with a guy wanting to get something cute for the babies?"

"First of all, nothing, but I never expected a guy like you to want to stop at a booth like that. Plus, you've never said the word *cute* in your life."

"A guy like me? What's a guy like me?"

"You know." She gestured at his appearance.

"Handsome? Debonair? Smoldering?" He tried his best to quirk his brow.

"A dude who handles hammers and horses, not hair bows."

"That's a lot of *H*s in that sentence."

"Here's another *H* word for you. It's hilarious, you saying 'cute.'"

"Get used to it, because Rose and Luna are the cutest cuties in Cute Town, and there's no comparable word in dudespeak that does them justice."

"Agreed." She laughed. "They don't need any more hair bows, though. They have plenty."

"Not with apples on them." He led her to a pair of bows fashioned of apple-patterned fabric. A tiny plastic apple surrounded by faux leaves had been sewn into the center. "The girls will look Foxtail official in those."

"You're right. Let's get them."

Wyatt pulled out his wallet.

The rest of the event passed in a blur. Natalie worked at the Foxtail booth while Wyatt spread a quilt on a dry patch of grass so Luna and Rose could stretch out. Later, while the girls slept in their stroller, he visited Willard Thibodeaux at the Happy Hooves paddock, finding himself checking out the mares. As he ran a hand down the flank of a gentle bay, Silas's careworn features crossed his mind. Silas always seemed engaged when Wyatt mentioned Beacon at their meetings. Maybe he should invite Silas to Manzanita Ranch for a ride. It would give them the opportunity to talk freely...or not talk, if that's what Silas preferred. It wouldn't hurt to ask.

A baby's squawk brought him back to the present. The event was winding down, so he took the girls with him to break down some of the Speed Dating areas. He hadn't done much work when Luna's chatter turned into a complaint, so he checked his watch. Lunchtime already?

"All right, let's get some food in your bellies."

He pushed the stroller to the volunteers' tent, where his parents had set out several pizza boxes from his favorite place in town, Pietro's, on a long table. The scents of onion, sausage and pepperoni made his mouth water.

Luna grumbled, as if she wanted some, too. He bent down to grab a small, soft-sided cooler from the stroller's storage basket. "You're too young yet for pizza, Lu-lu, but I have your lunch right here."

His mom rushed straight over, grinning at the babies. "Feeding time? Your dad and I can do it, Wyatt. Go get some pizza before it's gone."

Sure enough, a swarm of volunteers was streaming into the tent. He had work to do before he ate, though. He pulled out Ranger's travel water bottle and the girls' lunches. "I can wait. You two should eat."

"I snagged a piece of pepperoni already. Shh, don't tell anyone." Mom took a bib from his hand and snapped it around Luna's neck. "Go on, honey. We're fine here."

"Thanks, Mom. I'll be right back," he promised the girls.

Luna ignored him, making a loud, hungry noise as she watched his mom open the container of pureed squash and chicken.

"Hey, Wyatt." Thatcher stood at the end of the food line. "Not sure if you're interested, but I'm going hiking tomorrow morning with some guys if you'd like to join."

"Thanks, but tomorrow's Sunday. Church, with a potluck afterward. If hiking falls through, you're welcome to join us. I have no idea what I'll be bringing, but Natalie mentioned rolls, Sadie's bringing bean salad and Mick will probably bring pizza left over from this." He gestured around, laughing.

"Thanks, but the hiking plan is solid." Thatcher's dark brows knit. "You didn't used to attend church. You're different now, and I get that it's been a while since I've seen you, but I wondered…what got you going to church in the first place?"

Wyatt's jaw clamped shut so fast his teeth made a snapping sound. Not because he was ashamed of his faith, but of how he'd gotten there. First, hitting rock bottom as an addict, then recognizing he needed help from others, and also from God. How could he share that without admitting to his addiction?

He didn't want to lie, so he shared part of the truth. "I admitted I was lost. Once I finally opened my eyes to look for Him, I realized He had been calling my name for a long time. I just hadn't been paying attention."

Thatcher's Adam's apple worked. "Since Forrest and Cady died, I've had some questions. Maybe church has the answers."

"I recently joined a men's breakfast Bible study. Mick is in it, too. We meet at 6:00 a.m. at Trixie's Café, once a week. You're welcome to join us, even just to check it out and order some of Trixie's killer *huevos rancheros*. The house-made flour tortillas and salsa are worth getting out of bed early for."

A cowbell jangled, interrupting the conversations flowing through the tent. Wyatt turned around to see Mick, the large bell in hand, standing at the far end of the tent. "Your attention, please. First, thank you all for being here. Thanks to your hard work, nineteen animals found forever homes today." Mick's voice boomed through the tent. "Sixteen dogs, two cats and a rabbit."

The group broke into cheers.

"There are still a few animals left in the shelter, and more will inevitably be coming," Mick continued, "which is a reminder that our work never stops. But for right now, we want to celebrate you, our volunteers, for making My Furry Valentine such a success!"

"Thanks for the pizza!" Dove yelled.

"We've got more than just pizza for you all." Mick beckoned to Sadie, who trotted to his side carrying two baskets, each holding what looked like white papers. "Thanks to some generous donors in the community, there are prizes for a few of you. Shall we randomly select the winners?"

The cheers started again. Did the noise bother the babies? It didn't look like it. Luna was happily eating, Rose was ignoring the spoon in Dad's hand to watch the goings-on and even Ranger looked relaxed. Natalie had joined his parents, her eyes on the girls, smiling indulgently.

Thatcher's nudge drew him back to his surroundings. "If there are doughnuts in there, I hope I win them."

"What's with you and doughnuts lately?"

"First up," Mick called. "Sadie, what's the prize?"

Sadie pulled a paper out of the first basket and opened

it. "A gift card to Sarah's Ceramic Studio on Main Street! And the winner is…"

Mick pulled a paper from the second basket. "Bliss Anderson."

"Woot!" A young woman with cropped hair hopped from her seat and ran forward to claim her prize.

As more prizes were distributed, Wyatt and Thatcher moved up the line and filled their plates. They sat at the table with his family, Natalie, Dove and the babies. Wyatt sat beside Natalie, exchanging small smiles. Then he bent toward her. "I'll wolf these down, and then we should probably get the girls home. It's been a big day, and I have a feeling they'll want to crash for their afternoon naps early."

"I was thinking the same thing—"

"…here's the last one. Dinner for two at the Hollow," Sadie announced.

The nicest restaurant in town. Candlelit, romantic, always excellent. And the place where Wyatt got down on bended knee after dessert one date night and proposed to Natalie.

His mouth went dry.

"We'll pick a special winner for this one. Or should I say winners," Mick amended. He pulled a paper out from a bag Wyatt hadn't previously noticed in the basket. "Natalie Dalton and Wyatt Teague. Congratulations, you two!"

Wyatt's heart flopped around his stomach. Or maybe his pizza rebelled. Either way, his insides were quaking, but on the outside, he was still as a stone. Natalie didn't move, either.

"This is a setup," he muttered.

Natalie's nod was slight, but it was clear she agreed.

"I'll babysit." Sadie rushed toward them with the prize envelope.

"Me too," Dove added. "You have reservations—I mean,

the Hollow books up so quickly that we made reservations for whomever the winner is for two Fridays from now, six o'clock."

Folks in the room clapped. Everyone looked at them with expectant gazes.

Wyatt forced a smile so he wouldn't look ungrateful, even though he wanted to offer the prize back. Natalie wouldn't want to go there, of all places, with him of all people. Things were friendlier with them now, sure, but reliving the most romantic evening in their history by revisiting the site of his proposal?

Ugh.

He took the gift card and stretched his lips wider. "Thank you. This is so generous."

His mom beamed. "This is great. You two deserve a date night."

"It won't be a date," Natalie blurted.

The table went quiet. Wyatt scrambled to cover the awkwardness. "It'll be a much-appreciated night out. Adult conversation and food, nothing strained or pureed on the table."

"The Hollow's whipped potatoes are sort of pureed, if you think about it," his dad joked. Thankfully, it broke the tension.

Thatcher reached for his final slice of pizza. "Their prime rib is top-notch."

"Have you tried the lobster bisque?" His mom leaned toward Dove. "Scrumptious."

Wyatt turned his chair toward Natalie so he could speak privately. "We don't have to do this if you don't want to."

"Our families obviously pitched in for this and didn't think we would accept it unless we won it as a prize. How can we say no?" She glanced at him. "I think we're jelly belly."

Jelly belly—a code they'd invented years ago to mean they were trapped in a situation. They had been at some party, he couldn't remember whose now, and ended up staying later than they intended. Once they finally left and got into his truck, she'd apologized for being stuck in a conversation.

Stuck? Wyatt had teased her. Oh, how he had loved to tease her.

Stuck, she'd teased back. *Caught. No way out. In a jam.*

He couldn't remember which one of them was silly enough to go from jam to *jelly*, which somehow, ridiculously, led to *jelly belly*, but it became a private joke, trivial and at the same time precious, because it belonged to them alone. Part of their world of two.

He had loved those inside jokes. The intimacies of a private language budding from the experiences they shared as a loving couple.

Until he threw it all away for a handful of pills.

Natalie leaned into him. "We'll make the best of it."

Wow, did that sound unconvincing. Wyatt took it in stride. He didn't deserve better from her, after all he had put her through. "You'll have a decent evening, I promise."

But maybe it could be more than that, too. They couldn't go back in time, but this might be an opportunity to reconnect on some level, where they could find something more to base their relationship on than Rose and Luna. A new foundation, like the concrete that had been poured beneath the cabin site. Their relationship would never be the same, but that didn't mean it couldn't be good. Especially with the Lord at the center.

Their romantic relationship was long over, but it would sure be easier to raise the girls together if she actually started to like him again.

Chapter Six

It's not a date.

On Friday afternoon two weeks later, Wyatt stood in the grooming bay at Manzanita Ranch, brushing Beacon down after a ride while Ranger watched from a comfortable-looking spot atop a tuft of hay. A gentle rain freshened the world outside, and the barn was a hub of activity, with Mick tending to a gelding's tendinitis in the box and Wyatt's dad in the tack room, singing along to the vintage country tune on the radio while he oiled a saddle. The scents of rain, horse and leather paired with the tinny sound of the radio made Wyatt feel young again. It was just like old times.

Except back in those old times when Wyatt spent time with Beacon, he wasn't as nervous as a kid about his dinner at the Hollow tonight. Nor was he fresh from a meeting with fellow addicts. These past few weeks, however, secretly attending a meeting at the rec center before riding Beacon had become a pattern.

A positive pattern, one that made him feel stronger. There was something about the combination of support from others, paired with prayer and time on the back of a horse with his dog trotting alongside, that settled him. Redirected his thoughts and calmed him down like nothing else. Many aspects of Wyatt's life were uncertain, but there was no denying the sense of peace that descended over him when he was blessed to be out with Beacon.

That's why he had invited Silas to ride a few times these past few weeks. Silas seemed to enjoy the horses, too, and the time together deepened their burgeoning friendship.

The song on the radio faded out and Wyatt's dad appeared in the aisle, rag in hand. "Wyatt, thanks for cleaning the gutters earlier. It turned out to be perfect timing, with this unexpected rain shower."

"My pleasure, Dad." Wyatt had installed the gutters on the stables five years ago, but wind from the recent storm had dislodged a few sections and clogged the downspouts with debris. Standing water around the stables wasn't good for the horses. "It hardly took any time at all."

Dad tossed the oily rag into a bucket, then bent to pet Ranger. "You're always at your most natural when you're astride a horse or have a hammer in your hand."

Two things he hadn't done at all since following his job out of town, but now that he was back? He rode Beacon as often as possible, and he hauled out his tool belt to tackle repairs around Foxtail and Forrest and Cady's house while the girls slept.

Horses and hammers were easy for him. The rest of life, like navigating a world without his dear friends in it, figuring out how to best raise their girls, and attempting to be friends with Natalie again? Not so much.

"I'm just glad I could help." Wyatt gently touched the healed-up site of Beacon's scrape. "And I'm glad you got the roof on the storage barn fixed, too, Dad. Hopefully that's the last thing around here that's in need of repair from the big storm."

Mick stopped midstride as he passed the grooming bay, carrying his equine vet kit. "Plenty of things around town are still coming back together, slowly but surely." His brows rose as if he were talking about a mystery.

Wyatt wasn't great at riddles. "What do you mean?"

"You and Natalie," Dad interjected. "You've got that date at the Hollow tonight."

"It's not a date." Wyatt forced back a frustrated groan. If he admitted that Natalie viewed this evening as something to tolerate rather than enjoy, it would sound ungrateful to Mick, who'd contributed toward the gift, so he would keep mum on that aspect. "There's nothing between me and Natalie like…that."

"So, you're not getting back together?" Mick arched a brow at him.

"Of course not." A pang shot through him. "We've set aside our differences for the girls, and we need to get along if we're going to raise them as co-guardians. Don't read into it."

Dad's thick brows knit. "I guess that's true. Soon enough you'll hardly see each other, except to trade off the kids on the weekends."

Wyatt hated how that scenario made him feel, even if he couldn't name the emotions whirling like a hurricane in his gut. Rose and Luna were shaping his world in ways he never expected, and the thought of seeing far less of them than he was now—and Natalie, if he were honest—left a bitter taste in his mouth.

Ranger's soft muzzle nudged Wyatt's fist. He hadn't realized he'd clenched his hands until now, but his arms relaxed as he began stroking Ranger's soft head. The dog's ability to pick up on stress and anxiety—before Wyatt himself was often aware—was something.

And an opportune reminder to pray for God's strength before he got too upset or tempted to think about how easy it would be to return to his addiction. *Thanks for this les-son, Lord.*

Wyatt felt his pulse slow, then looked at his father. "Splitting custody like that is the best plan we've come up with so far, but the truth is, I don't like it much. I've asked my boss for permission to work remotely one or two days a week so I can be in town more, but even that doesn't feel like enough. I would rather be with the girls every day."

Mick zipped up his kit bag. "Why don't you move back and branch out on your own? Start an architecture firm here?"

Before Wyatt could answer, his dad snorted. "Golden-rod is too small, too saturated for another architect. No, as much as you want to be part of the girls' daily lives, it's not realistic. Natalie is stuck here due to her father's will, and you would be a fool to give up your career in Irvine. You've got to provide for those girls somehow."

But what would life look like if he could provide for them here, in Goldenrod?

It was, as his dad said, unrealistic. But that didn't mean it was impossible. God's solution to this mess might be un-expected, perhaps even greater than Wyatt could imagine. He would do well to wait on the Lord.

No matter what his dad said about it.

"I'm not sure what's going to happen yet, Dad, but I trust that God is going to work this out."

Dad's expression was doubtful. "I hope it gets worked out fast, then, seeing as the court-appointed inspector is coming on Monday, isn't she? You'll have to tell her some-thing about your plans."

A wave of frustration rose in Wyatt, and he countered it with a prayer. *Help me to wait on You, Lord.*

"I'm praying for the situation." Mick looked like he

wanted to say more but thought the better of it. His gaze hadn't missed Ranger's proximity to Wyatt, though. Did his cousin realize there was more going on with Wyatt than general stress? "In the meantime, don't you have a date—er, non-date to get ready for?"

Wyatt hoped his cousin could read his gratitude in his eyes. "Yeah, I'd better get going. Is it okay if I leave Ranger here?"

"Of course." Dad grinned. "We're good buddies."

Wyatt started to unclip Beacon, but Mick stayed him with a hand. "I've got him. No offense, but you need a shower before you pick up Natalie."

Dad waved. "Enjoy your date."

"It's not a date, Dad." Wyatt patted his dad's back before leaving the stable.

But it sure felt like one as he showered and donned a crisply ironed button-down, tan chinos and his good boots. A shiver of nerves skittered in his gut as he drove to Forrest and Cady's house to pick up Natalie. *It's just dinner.* A night out, gifted by their friends. Just like Natalie had said, *we'll make the best of it.*

It's not a date.

He repeated it to himself as he climbed up the porch steps and rang the bell. Natalie answered the door, wearing a tentative smile and a dark green dress that was modest but accentuated her slim figure just right.

It wasn't the dress or the loose waves in her shiny hair or the subtle makeup that made her beautiful to him, though—not in the past, and not now—but the joyful, radiant look in her eye that robbed him of breath. She was stunningly, achingly gorgeous.

He couldn't speak. Even to remind himself that this was absolutely, positively not a date.

We'll make the best of it. Forget that. How was he going to get through the evening without wanting to kiss her?

"Here's to making the best of an awkward situation." Natalie lifted her minty limeade in a toast, clinking her glass against Wyatt's soda.

His hand went to his heart as if she'd mortally wounded him, but his crooked smile told her he would live. "Come on now, the evening hasn't been that bad, has it?"

"No, it hasn't." She took a sip of her drink, savoring the tart mingling with the sweet. Delicious, just as their appetizer of sausage-stuffed mushrooms had been. Now, their twentysomething server with a thin mustache delivered their entrées.

As if by unspoken agreement, their conversation had steered clear of Wyatt's proposal here or any memories associated with it. They had both ordered different items than they had that fateful night, and they discussed light topics, including the girls' antics and how well the cabin was progressing.

But as she picked up her dinner fork, Natalie had to admit something. "I wasn't sure this was the best idea, but it is nice to get out of the house and enjoy such a delicious meal. And you always did clean up well."

After the words came out of her mouth, she wanted to bite her tongue. Complimenting his appearance was not something she had planned to do this evening, but mercy, did he look good in that pale blue shirt. The fabric stretched just so, accentuating his strong shoulders and arms.

She couldn't ignore the subtle but unmistakable scent of the cedar aftershave, either. Back in the day, he always used it on their date nights, and his freshly shaven jaw and cheeks practically begged her palm to gauge their smoothness.

She took a gulp of her mocktail.

She shouldn't—wouldn't—think that way about him anymore, but...they were sitting in a U-shaped booth in a candlelit restaurant. They had a romantic past.

And Wyatt seemed determined to set her at ease, keeping the conversation relaxed and upbeat. Things were so easy between them tonight, it reminded her of the countless happy times they'd shared. Not just the night he proposed in this very restaurant, but the everyday things. Like their private jokes. How it felt to snuggle beneath his shoulder. How his kiss made her breathless—

"I was going to say the same thing," he said, breaking her reverie. "You look lovely tonight."

"Thanks." She decided to return to the light tone they had been enjoying before she'd slipped up and blurted how handsome he was. "I've got to say, this risotto is something to dress up for."

"I'm glad you're enjoying it." His eyes gleamed in the light of the flickering votive candles set on the table. "The past few weeks have been difficult, no question. Our lives have been turned upside down, but a lot of people pitched in so we could have a small break tonight, and I'm grateful."

"You're right. This is a lavish gift from people who care about us. We shouldn't waste it."

"That means dessert, you know."

She'd seen the gift card, and while it was generous, they had probably spent more than it covered already. "I'm not sure dessert is in the budget."

"Nah, the rest of the tab is on me. In fact, I'm ashamed I didn't take you out before now."

"I wouldn't have said yes if it hadn't been forced on me." It was the truth, but she coated it in a teasing tone.

Thankfully, he laughed. "Because you wouldn't want to leave the girls, of course. Right?"

That wasn't her reason, but it was valid. "We have been the ones to put Rose and Luna to bed every night for over a month now. I've worried they might get upset tonight that at least one of us isn't there."

"Sadie and Dove can handle a little fussing. And if something happens and your sisters need us, they will call or text, and we'll be home in record time." His innocent expression didn't fool her a whit, though. He knew perfectly well she wouldn't go out to dinner with him because she was afraid to be alone with him.

It wasn't because she hated him. Far from it. She still struggled to trust him, but that wasn't the reason, either.

It was because she wasn't sure who they were without the babies in the room.

The past year, she'd clung to her resentment toward him, over how he'd chosen his job over her, left her the way he did. What would it be like if she let that resentment go?

The idea sent her into a mild panic, because if she did that, it would feel like she was okay with what he had done. She would never be okay with it, ever.

But that didn't mean she shouldn't—couldn't—forgive him. Especially because she knew, deep down, that forgiving Wyatt wasn't about condoning his actions, but rather refusing to hold them against him for the rest of their lives. She wouldn't treat his decision to move to Irvine like a rock in her pocket, rubbing her fingers over it when she wanted to feel justified or pulling it out when she needed to score points during an argument.

Just like how God didn't view her through her offenses.

Forgive others just as God forgave you... Her women's

Bible study had covered that last week. It hadn't hit her as hard then as it did now, though.

Maybe it was time to forgive him.

For his sake as well as her own, and certainly for the babies'. It would require a conversation, but this wasn't the time or place. Perhaps the best way to move forward, for now, was to stop overthinking, set aside her questions and doubts, and take steps toward being friendly.

Maybe even friends. And she might just enjoy herself tonight in the process.

She lifted her drink and met his gaze over the rim. "So, how exhausted do you think Dove and Sadie are, on a scale from one to ten, now that Rose and Luna are crawling?"

"Eleven. Rose is fast. Like, bullet train fast."

"Luna's slower, but she always seems to go right where I don't want her to."

"Like that one cupboard we forgot to put a safety lock on." Wyatt sliced into his pork loin. "Or Ranger's slobbery toys."

"Or the hammer you set down on the coffee table after rehanging that picture that fell in the living room."

"Yeah, thankfully I learned that lesson before Rose got a grip on it."

Natalie forked her risotto. "We're not used to little hands getting into everything, but we need to prepare. It's going to be more challenging once they start walking."

"And climbing things." Wyatt smiled as if he were remembering something. "Like the fridge."

"They won't— Oh, no, you climbed the refrigerator when you were little, didn't you?" Natalie's stomach swooped at the thought of Rose and Luna that high off the ground.

"My mom found me sitting on top of it when I was maybe two." His shrug was nonchalant, as if a toddler atop an appliance was no big deal. "I have no memory of that incident, but I do remember getting stitches more than once. And then there was that time Mick and I jumped from the barn loft into a haystack. We both spent the summer with casts on our arms."

"I've never heard that story." And they'd known each other since they were in their early teens.

He shrugged. "It was all normal kid stuff."

"Not for me and my sisters. Maybe climbing like that is a boy thing?" Her tone was hopeful.

Wyatt just laughed. But Natalie was resolved. There would be no climbing appliances in her house.

Their conversation flowed as smoothly as a stream through the rest of dinner, dessert and the ride back to the house in Wyatt's truck. Sitting in the cab with him for an evening ride, streetlights reflecting on the dashboard and the scents of leather and his aftershave in the air, all brought back memories of years' worth of date nights, holding his right hand while he drove with his left.

Tonight, both of his hands were securely placed on the wheel, at ten and two. Just like he had surely been taught in driver's education class back in high school.

Which gave her a startling thought. "I just realized we have to teach Rose and Luna to drive in, what, fifteen years? I'm already petrified."

"And excited." Wyatt turned onto their street. "It's a rite of passage, and it'll be fun."

Would it? "My mom screeched a lot, teaching me."

"She taught you? I always assumed your dad was taking you on dirt roads at the orchard."

"Nope." She and Wyatt must have never talked about it when they were younger. They met before they could drive, but by the time they began to date, they must have both had their licenses. "It would have been a good idea, though. I wouldn't have been in danger of hitting anything. Did you practice out on the ranch?"

"On the perimeter roads, yeah. We'll do that with Rose and Luna, get them comfortable behind the wheel before we take them out on city streets. Look at us, planning all of this fifteen years ahead of schedule."

Part of her brain screamed that she and Wyatt still didn't know how they were going to raise the girls together. Where he would live. Where she'd live, since her dad's will stated she had to live at Foxtail Farm for another four years, and the lawyer had said she could alternate nights at Forrest and Cady's temporarily, not permanently. She could move the girls into her apartment with her, but it was so small, she wasn't sure how they'd make it work…

She kicked those thoughts to the curb. At least for the moment. She didn't want to ruin such a pleasant evening. It was more fun than she'd had in, well, nearly a year. Since Wyatt had left.

This was exactly like old times, and she didn't want it to end.

Wyatt pulled into the driveway beside her SUV, cutting the engine and making no move to get out. Maybe he didn't want this evening to end, either.

Releasing his seat belt, he turned toward her, a gleam in his eye. "When the girls do eventually drive, what sort of car should they have at their disposal? Because I'm thinking they should share an armored tank."

She snickered. "Like an army tank?"

"Exactly. Nothing can hurt 'em that way."

She used to love their silly conversations like this. "And if they're late for school, they can just drive off road?"

"Right through the trees. Over other cars, even." His

lips curved in the most appealing way. "Shave some time off the route."

"And where will you get this tank? I'm not sure they're available for civilian purchase."

"I work with wood, not metal, but I figure it couldn't be too hard to make."

"A homemade tank. I'm sure they'll be the envy of everyone at school." Picturing the ridiculousness of it, she laughed.

"Natalie." His smile fell. Not in a way that was sad or upset. More serious. "You are so...so..."

His pause was so long, she had to tease him. "I'm so-so? Thanks. So-so. Wow."

He didn't tease back. His eyes were liquid black in the dim yellow light streaming from the front porch into the truck cab, and his breadth seemed to fill the space.

"You're so lovely," he murmured.

Somewhere in the back of her mind, a faint warning sounded. So distant, it was easy to ignore. The magnetic force of his gaze drew her toward him.

"Wyatt." His name came out in a whisper. Soft as breath.

His gaze dropped from her eyes to her lips. He wanted to kiss her, then. She shouldn't, but she wanted it, too.

She closed the distance between them, and then his lips were on hers, gentle, testing her reaction. When she didn't pull back, his arms went around her, strong and warm, and he deepened the kiss.

Oh, how she'd missed him, no matter how hard she'd denied it. His lightness when she was too serious, his banter and ease. And she missed being close to him. Held by him, feeling protected, treasured.

He pulled back, staring down at her in wonder. It felt unreal, like a dream, and she never wanted to wake up.

But this is no dream. And—

Reality washed over her like a cold ocean wave in winter. Their relationship was not about just them anymore.

She forced herself to inch away from him. "That was lovely, Wyatt, but I— It was a mistake. I don't deny I wanted to, but I think it best if we don't repeat it. There's too much at stake, with the girls."

A shadow fell over his features, but he let her go. "Agreed. We can forget it happened."

There was no way she was going to forget it, even if she lived to be a hundred and ten, but she gathered her purse from the floor. "We should probably go in." It was her night to stay with the babies, but as she expected, Wyatt got out of the truck with her.

He took a deep, shaky breath. "I admit, I'm curious to know how the girls did with your sisters."

Hopefully Dove and Sadie wouldn't be able to tell they had kissed just by looking at them. Her fingers went to her lips, grateful she had swiped on a twelve-hour-stain lipstick. It was a darker shade than she usually wore, but when Dove had handed her the tube after seeing her in this green dress, she had to admit the look bolstered her confidence for this…nondate.

Nondate. With kissing. Ugh, what had she done?

Dove met them at the front door, her grin eager. "How was your dinner?"

"Great. How were the girls?"

Dove's lips mashed in a disappointed-looking pout. "Glad the food was adequate. The girls were perfect, though."

Abashed by her lack of raving over their experience at the Hollow, Natalie made a show of rubbing her stomach as they entered the house. "Our dinner was perfect, too.

The risotto was so creamy and rich. And even though I was stuffed, I still managed to put away a whole crème brûlée."

"Oh, those are my favorite." Sadie joined them in the hall and reached for her coat. "How was your dinner, Wyatt?"

"Awesome, as expected. Thanks so much for everything. The card, the babysitting, all of it." He sounded so casual, no one would ever guess they'd just shared a kiss.

Maybe it hadn't affected him, though. Well, it sure had Natalie.

After a few minutes' talk about the food and the babies' antics before bed, her sisters left. In an attempt to behave normally around Wyatt—normal meaning friendly, as if the kiss hadn't happened—Natalie took a step toward the kitchen to initiate their nightly routine. "I'll grab my tea and your decaf while you check on the girls. Do you want sugar, after our super-sweet desserts?"

Wyatt pulled his phone from his pocket, stared at the screen for a few seconds and then forced a smile. "No coffee, actually. I'd better go."

They always sat over a mug of something once the girls went to bed. "Did something happen?" She stared at his phone.

"No. It's just getting late. And tomorrow morning I have that online meeting with my boss, remember? Among other things, I'm going to present my prefab cabin idea. And you're meeting Dutch early, aren't you?"

The way he avoided her gaze, Natalie felt herself thrust back in time again, not to the happy days of their early courtship, but to the weeks before he left town, when he'd slowly but surely withdrawn from her.

"Those things are true, but I can't shake the feeling that you're lying to me." Natalie's hands went to her swirling stomach. "Is it because of what happened in the truck?"

His eyes shut for a moment. "You're the one who said it was a mistake."

"But I didn't say we should back off trying to find a sense of normalcy. Being a team for the girls' sakes."

A muscle twitched in the jaw she'd caressed mere minutes ago. "I'm not leaving because of the kiss."

"Is it the same reason you left town in the first place, then? The real reason? It is, isn't it? It's so obvious."

He froze, his eyes going wide. "You know?"

"It wasn't hard to figure out." She bent to gather the toys scattered across the floor, tossing them into the cream cloth basket by the couch so she didn't have to look him in the eye. "Your job came first. It was too easy of a choice for you, and when you realized that, it revealed to you that I wasn't that important to you anymore. You were too cowardly to admit it, though, and you wanted me to be the one to break up with you. Just like you're weirded out by our kiss now and would rather run away than face me."

So much for her choosing not to hold his role in their breakup against him. But how could she not bring it up when history was repeating itself?

"No, Nat."

"Yes." Just like her dad, making her feel loved with presents and hugs and happy summers at Foxtail Farm and then disappearing from her life the rest of the year. Not showing up to awards assemblies or returning phone calls or even sending child support regularly. Wyatt might not be the same as her dad in every way, but he was in this.

Untrustworthy. Gone when you needed them most. And she would not allow that to happen to Rose and Luna. "Don't forget, you've made promises to stay in the girls' lives. If you want out, say so now, before we meet with the judge, because I won't let you commit to the girls and then run from them the way you ran from me."

"Natalie, I didn't want to leave just now because of the kiss. This is not like our breakup." He glanced at his phone, grimaced and then gripped it tightly. "If I can just have a minute to sort something out—"

"You have a girlfriend, don't you?" She blurted it out. "Alex. I've seen the text alerts you get from her. I'm not trying to spy or anything, but sometimes, they're just there."

He glanced up. "Alex is not my girlfriend. Neither is the person I'm texting. And I haven't kissed anyone else but you in my life. Or remotely wanted to."

She shouldn't feel relieved, but she couldn't help it. Other than that, the only thing that registered was confusion. "If Alex isn't your girlfriend, who is she?"

"He." Wyatt shoved the phone in his pocket. "A friend." He ran a hand through his hair, as if unsure what to say next, but then he met her gaze squarely. "And the person I'm texting asked if I was free to meet up now to talk. I thought maybe I should go—but I fumbled this, and being with you right now is more important. He's going to reach out to someone else from our group to talk."

"It's an emergency? Just go then, but…someone in your men's Bible study group is in trouble?" That was the only group he belonged to that she knew of. "Who is it? What's wrong?"

"Not that type of group." He let out a long breath and met her gaze. "I didn't leave town because I didn't want to marry you, Natalie. Or because my job is more important than you. I left because I'm an addict."

Chapter Seven

Natalie's breath stuck somewhere under her rib cage. How— what— *Okay, just breathe.*

There. In and out, deep and even, using her stomach muscles to help calm her body. After a few breaths, her thoughts became more coherent, but that didn't mean Wyatt's words made any sense to her. "Are you talking about a recovery support group? I don't understand. You've never touched alcohol or substances. Ever."

Wyatt gestured for her to sit down, and she dropped into one of the chairs by the empty fireplace. He sat opposite, exactly where he sat the night of the funeral. "Remember when I hurt my back on the construction site?"

"Of course." Over a year ago.

"The doctor prescribed physical therapy and, at the beginning, opioid painkillers. Before I knew it, I was dependent on them."

Impossible. "That's the sort of thing I would notice."

Her words hung in the air a moment before Wyatt shook his head. "I did a good job of hiding it. I was high functioning. Never missed work, and no one suspected."

"Yeah, but we were engaged. I saw you daily." How could she not have seen the signs?

She scanned memories of that time. Wyatt was injured

before Christmas. Then, in January, her dad died, leaving a will so demanding that it almost seemed like a cruel joke instead of a legacy. Although she'd already worked at the Foxtail Farm office, her dad's will thrust her into new roles she hadn't felt equipped to handle, including managing Thatcher, Sadie and Dove. And accounting. Organization was her strong suit, but when it involved math, she was not at her best.

It wasn't long after that when Wyatt began a quiet but steady retreat from her. He bowed out of plans, claiming busyness or fatigue, and he seemed preoccupied when they were together. When they were apart, he took longer and longer to return her calls and texts. At the time, she had never thought to ask him why, because she figured she already knew the answer.

Agony pooled in her belly. "I guess I did notice some signs. But opioids?" She knew they were highly addictive, but she had never thought addiction would touch anyone in her sphere.

Or that when it did she wouldn't have figured it out immediately.

It wasn't that simple, though. Their relationship had had problems even before Wyatt hurt his back. Their differences in temperament sometimes brought balance—as it had on the night of the funeral when little Rose screamed, and Wyatt's calm countered Natalie's panic—but more often, their differences caused clashes. He didn't always understand her need for organization, and she… Well, Wyatt clearly didn't feel he could confide in her, since he'd chosen to leave her without being truthful about why.

Just like when her dad left her mom, lying that there wasn't anyone else, when Natalie was six years old.

Despite confusion and guilt roiling inside of her, questions pushed to the surface like bubbles in a boiling kettle.

"I loved you. You said you loved me, too, but you let me believe a lie. Didn't I warrant the respect, the courtesy, of the truth?"

"That wasn't it at all." Wyatt's face was sad. "I was trying to protect you."

"That's plumb idiotic. Protect me by telling me lies?"

"I told myself you had too much on your plate, losing your dad and trying to get Foxtail Farm on track."

"Feeble excuses, Wyatt."

"You're right. The real reason I left was because you deserved a whole man, not a broken one. When the firm announced plans to relocate, I thought if I temporarily moved with them and got treatment, I could return home all fixed, once I figured out how to make a living back here in Goldenrod. I would move back to town and you would never have known anything was wrong." He leaned forward, resting his elbows on his knees. "You're not the only one who thinks I'm an idiot. Alex has been after me to tell you and my parents—"

"Wait, Gary and Jillian don't know?"

"No one knew but Forrest and Cady. Not even Mick." He puffed out his breath. "How could I tell my family that I had messed up so badly? I was a complete wreck, and they wouldn't have understood."

"They're such kind people. They might struggle at first, but they love you. And they're such positive people." She'd always liked that about them. No drama, no raised voices.

"They do love me, but their 'positivity' is more about looking perfect than having real peace. If others don't see my family go through trials or heavy emotions, it's not because the Teagues don't have them. It's because we learned to shove our struggles beneath the rug rather than share them. That's why I wanted to go to rehab, clean up and come back with no one the wiser about me leaving for anything other than my job. I wouldn't have disappointed my parents, you, anyone. Life would be normal again."

She shook her head. "I don't think life will ever be back to that old normal. Not for any of us."

"It was a foolish hope—I know that now. And I'm glad now that some things have changed. I used to think my more negative feelings were shameful, but now I see their worth as God-given and not a weakness. Until I left, I never knew how unhealthily I dealt with stress, because I always felt the pressure to be successful, to have my act together."

"I'm sorry, Wyatt. For being your fiancée, I sure was oblivious to a lot of things you were going through."

"That's over, though, and I want to forge a new normal for Rose and Luna, founded on our faith. I don't ever want to do anything that could jeopardize my guardianship. They're more than enough motivation to walk the straight and narrow."

He was fighting for the babies. How could she argue with that? But still, questions swirled in her head. "Is that why you didn't tell me the truth when you first came back? Did you think I would fight you on custody?"

"Not so much that as—I just wish I hadn't messed up at all, so it would never be a factor in anyone's mind, if that makes sense. I didn't want one more obstacle in the way of us moving forward in all of this. It's tough enough between us as it is, considering our past. And I was ashamed." He tipped his head to peer at her. "I'll be forthright from here on out, so you know when I attend meetings, that sort of thing. And I'll be open during the home visit with the investigator. I don't want to hide anything. All I ask is that

I'm the one to tell my family myself. When I feel the time is right."

"Of course."

"I hurt you, Natalie, and I'm sorry. At the very least, I owe you answers to any questions you may have, now or in the future. I know it's a lot to process."

"There is one thing I want to ask now. Are you okay?" It felt like a dumb thing to ask, but he had obviously been through a lot.

A smile softened his serious features. "Better than okay. I go to meetings, as I mentioned. That's how I met Alex. Awesome dude who works in the construction industry, so we have a lot in common. Same with the guy who was texting me earlier—we all hold each other accountable. And now, I have newfound faith in the One who can give me strength to uphold my sobriety. I don't ever want to go back to the way I was before I met Him."

Natalie's hand rested atop her beating heart. "I wondered why you started going to church. I thought Mick might have encouraged you the way Sadie encouraged me. I started going to church with her a few weeks after you left. I needed… Him." His unconditional love. His promise to never abandon her the way the important men in her life had seemed to do.

"God certainly used our difficulties to draw us to Himself. I wish it hadn't taken so much for me to pay attention to Him, though." Wyatt leaned back, meeting her gaze squarely. "I lost your trust. I don't deserve it, but I'm going to do everything I can to earn it back, Nat. I promise."

Natalie stared down at her hands, folded neatly on her lap. As much as she appreciated Wyatt's reliance on God, his commitment to the babies and his good intentions, it might not be enough for her. Not because he could someday slip up, but because the faith she'd once had in him had sustained a painful injury. There was a scar, but sometimes the wound still felt like it hadn't healed.

Now she better understood why he left—and yes, she hadn't known all the facts when she'd issued the ultimatum that ended their engagement—but underlying it all was the deep, aching fear that she shouldn't—couldn't—count on anyone. Not her father, who confused and hurt her in life and left no closure in his death. Not her mom, whose bitterness against Dad caused guilt and grief in her children. Not her sisters, because she had always led them in a pseudo-parental role rather than growing up alongside them as equals.

And not Wyatt, because he'd left her.

So she had to be honest. "I'm not sure how or if I can ever trust you again, Wyatt."

Wyatt wasn't surprised by Natalie's statement that she might never be able to rely on him again. She probably didn't realize how tightly she clung to control in an attempt to ward off pain, and he couldn't blame her, considering he'd caused a large percentage of her anguish.

But that didn't mean he wasn't sincere. He stared into her beautiful, sad eyes. "My word might not mean much to you, but I hope time will prove my faithfulness. In the meantime, I will finish the cabin and demonstrate that I'm sober, to you and the court. I can provide my rehab certification and meeting attendance, go through regular screenings, anything you want. And don't forget my online meeting with Solomon tomorrow, where I'm pressing for his permission to work remotely. Since I proposed adding cabin styles to the firm's catalog, I hope that gives him more incentive to say yes."

Her lower lip caught between her teeth, a sign she was thoughtful, but also a reminder that he'd been kissing those lips not long ago. Thinking there was a chance that things might be changing for the better between them.

That had lasted maybe five minutes, hadn't it?

She sighed. "I appreciate your willingness to prove your commitment to your sobriety. And to the girls. But trust is fragile, and I feel like I've been lied to."

"This has been a lot, I know."

"There's a lot to think about, but tomorrow is a new day. We'll go forward from here, with honesty."

"I can't ask for more." He wished he could hug her, but he kept his arms to himself when they stood up. "Thanks."

The drive home was cold but hopeful. Alex had been right—talking to Natalie about his addiction had lifted a weight off his shoulders that he hadn't realized he'd been carrying.

The next morning, Wyatt's sense of hope was still high as he drove to Forrest and Cady's, Ranger and his work bag at his side.

At the house, he knocked on the door and Natalie appeared, bundled against the crisp morning in a fluffy beige turtleneck sweater. "Come on in. It's cold."

Warmth soaked into his skin as the heater's blast rippled through the room. "I just heard on the radio that the temperature won't crack forty-five today. Good news for Foxtail." He had learned a lot about apples in their time together, and chilly winter temperatures were essential for the tree to blossom in spring.

Natalie nodded. "What a strange, wet winter it has been."

Wyatt slipped out of his jacket and followed the baby coos into the living room, where both girls were playing atop blankets. He dropped to his stomach to greet them.

"Yi-yit." Rose's little legs kicked.

Surprise surged through him. "Did you just say Wyatt? Nat, she said my name."

"I think they're too young to have names for us." Natalie sat cross-legged with them. "She's probably just babbling."

True, Rose was spouting gibberish now, but Wyatt wouldn't be deterred. He playfully grabbed Rose's sock-clad toes. "Your first word was Wy-att, wasn't it, duck?"

"You're incorrigible. But two can play at that game." Natalie's lips twitched. "Can you say Nat-a-lee, girls? Nat-a-lee."

"Wy-att," he enunciated at Luna.

Luna blew a raspberry instead.

Wyatt's phone buzzed in his pocket. Rolling over, he tugged it free. When he read the message, his chest tightened. "It's Solomon. He wants to have our meeting in person."

Natalie froze. "Today?"

"As soon as I can get there, yeah." At least traffic wouldn't be as heavy since it was a Saturday, but the stretch of I-5 that ran through Marine Corps Base Camp Pendleton was always bad. "He says this is too big a conversation to have over a screen." Which didn't boost Wyatt's confidence when it came to his proposal to work remotely.

"Bad enough to meet on a Saturday, but to make you drive this far, last-minute? He's too demanding, Wyatt."

"And I'm supposed to have the girls so you can look over the new irrigation system with Dutch. I'll ask Solomon to reschedule."

"'No' doesn't tend to be a great thing to tell one's boss, though, does it?"

"I don't care. The girls come first, and technically, I'm still on family leave." He shifted position as Ranger snuggled alongside him. "I'm as upset about this as you are."

"I'm not upset."

He almost laughed, considering the tight edge in her voice, but that would make things worse. She rose and strode out of the room, a clear sign she didn't want to talk like this in front of the babies, and all he could do was follow her into the kitchen. He leaned against the counter, watching her pour hot water from the electric kettle into a mug. "I'll make some calls to find babysitting so you can work," he said. "We're a team, remember?"

"I don't know who you'd ask to babysit. Your parents are out of town and my sisters are operating the farm stand. Saturday is the busiest day of the week." She waved her hand. "It's fine. I just wish I had more notice. I'm trying to trust you, and now this happens."

He lost the ability to speak for a moment as her words cut through him like a dull knife. "How is this situation damaging my trustworthiness?"

"I didn't mean it like that."

"Are you sure? Because this is out of my control. I don't think I've done anything to cause you to question my commitment to the girls. The whole point of this meeting is so I can be here more. For them." He kept his voice low, his tone even, so the babies wouldn't hear their disagreement. "I'm not running away from anything."

Although, angry as he was, the idea of some time alone held appeal.

A warm, moist muzzle bumped against his left hand, accompanied by the weight of Ranger's body against Wyatt's leg, heavy and comforting. Wyatt let out a shaky breath and rubbed the dog's skull.

Natalie's gaze followed his hand. "He knows when… you need him."

The thought of needing anyone, anything, drew him up

short, only for him to realize it was true. In the past year, he had learned a hundred times over that seeking help was a sign of strength, not weakness, but his parents' voices in his head still didn't accept it.

Real men don't ask for help.

Only children can't control their emotions.

Get a grip, son, and turn that frown upside down.

All followed by a hasty change of subject.

But Natalie was right. Ranger knew just what he needed, and when. "He has been a gift from God when I feel…" Emotions were not his strong suit, not raised in the house he grew up in. "Angry."

"Tempted," Natalie suggested. "I don't mean that in a bad way, but last night I did some reading on addiction before I went to bed. It sounds like it's a lifetime struggle, especially when times get tough."

She didn't sound judgmental, but Wyatt shook his head. "No matter how hard life gets, I will never be tempted to go back to that nightmare, not when I have God. And friends like Alex and the support of the people in my group. But you might be right about sometimes wishing things were different. Like feeling I can never regain your trust."

Her eyes were moist. "I just don't like counting on something and then it disappears."

Like their relationship?

Hardly. She was talking about her expectations for the day.

"It's life, though. Especially with kids—we'll think we know what the day holds and then suddenly they'll need stitches or lose their homework or disagree with a friend, and everything else will stop to accommodate the unexpected course of the day."

"I know that, Wyatt." She dunked a tea bag into her mug,

spreading the fragrance of peppermint through the kitchen. "It's just that no one else seems to plan ahead for anything, and I'm left dealing with the fallout."

"I couldn't possibly have anticipated my boss's text."

"I guess we should have. It's better than feeling blind-sided."

"We can't prepare for every possible pitfall, Nat. And I said I would ask him to reschedule."

"No. This is an important meeting, so you have to go. Besides, I think we could both use some space. You're right, this isn't anyone's fault, but it still feels like I'm the one picking up the pieces."

No one's fault, yet they were nevertheless at odds. Wyatt returned to the living room, bent to kiss the girls' heads and whisper goodbye. Then he paused at the door, where Natalie stood, mug in hand, frowning.

"I would gladly pick up the pieces for you, Natalie. In fact, I thought that was what we've been doing for each other the last five weeks."

He shut the front door behind him, calling himself all kinds of a fool. The complications in their relationship seemed impossible to smooth. How were they ever going to get their act together enough to raise Rose and Luna to-gether?

Chapter Eight

That evening after dinner, Natalie stared out the rain-blurred front window, hands pressed against her stomach as if she could encapsulate the panic growing inside. The rain was heavier than forecast, and the wind howled as it swirled around the house and whipped through the trees.

Not as bad as the storm last month that caused so much damage, but bad enough to give her cause for concern. Weather like this could be dangerous, and the thought of Wyatt driving back to Goldenrod in it tonight made her stomach tighten.

No accidents, Lord. Please.

She didn't dare let her fear show, however. Not with Rose and Luna in the room, cuddling with Beatie on the couch over a toddler-appropriate Bible storybook.

"Ready to play?" The tone Beatie used only for the babies made Natalie turn around. Rose was shifting off the couch, followed by Luna and both guided by Beatie's loving hand. "I guess story time is over."

Natalie couldn't help but smile as the babies crawled toward the toddler kitchen they had received at her Bible study's baby shower. Luna immediately reached for the play saltshaker that sounded like a maraca when it moved, and Rose grasped the handle of one of the tiny pots.

Natalie looked at Beatie. "Thanks for spending the evening with us."

"Are you kidding? I got to play with the babies, and I know Dutch didn't miss me. Not when there's a basketball game on. So, what's so interesting out this window?" Beatie joined her, peering out at the dark street. "Everything's kind of blurry to me. I think I need new glasses."

"I'm not really looking at anything."

"Ah, but you're looking *for* something. Someone. If you're concerned about Wyatt, why don't you text him? His truck is new enough that it should have that hands-free doohickey feature so he can respond to you while he drives."

"I don't even know when he left Irvine for Goldenrod. *If* he left. He could have decided to meet his friend Alex for dinner."

Besides, the principle of the thing rankled. Shouldn't *he* have been the one to text *her* as a matter of common courtesy? Didn't he think about how the way the headlights turning into the neighborhood on a rainy evening would remind her of that awful night when she was babysitting Rose and Luna, and the police came to the house and told her Forrest and Cady were never coming home again?

Natalie turned away, reminding herself he had no way of knowing that. She couldn't expect him to read her mind.

He had mentioned their issues with miscommunication earlier today. How much of it had to do with her pride? She picked at a loose thread on her sweater cuff. "Maybe I'll text or call later if I don't hear anything soon."

"I take it you two had a spat before he left."

"Is it that obvious?"

"You've been quiet all afternoon." Beatie shrugged. "No judgment from me. It's not a bad thing to let off steam from time to time. Keeps the pot from boiling over, if you know what I mean."

"I never thought of it that way. We never fought much until…well, until the pot boiled over."

"Your parents weren't exactly models in that department, if you'll forgive my saying so. The way Yvonne and Asa bickered, you probably grew up thinking that happy people never disagree. Then you met Wyatt, from a family that never said a negative word. Must've seemed ideal to you."

Natalie bit her lip. "I did always love that about the Teagues." But she hadn't understood that troubles were hidden away, ignored like messes in the back corner of a closet. "Everything looked perfect."

"Nothing's perfect, sweetheart."

"I know. I just wanted something closer to it than what I had growing up." Still wanted it. To raise happy, healthy girls and utilize all the potential Foxtail Farm had to support their family. Wanted to see her future smooth and flat ahead of her, like that long section of Route 66 through the desert of New Mexico she had driven when she was sixteen with her mom and sisters, visiting relatives in Colorado. Where she could see everything coming, no surprises.

A shrill beep screeched from Natalie's phone. Then Beatie's. At once, Luna began to fuss. Natalie scooped up the baby and then grabbed her phone from the coffee table. She'd received one of these alerts the night of the big storm, and the sound made her pulse skitter.

"What is that?" Beatie dug into her purse.

"A weather and traffic alert. It says there has been an accident somewhere in town." Nausea roiled her stomach, and her hands were shaking so hard she could barely scan through the alert for more information.

"Where? I can't make out all of the words." Beatie lifted her head to peer beneath her glasses at the screen.

"I don't know." Then she pressed a kiss onto Luna's curls. "Shh, baby, I know that was a scary noise, but it's okay." Great, now she was lying to the baby, because it wasn't okay at all. Not with Wyatt driving in the heavy rain and wind.

Worst-case scenarios came into her thoughts far too easily, and it was difficult for her to stop. She asked God for help and resolved to think positively. *Not just positively, but biblically. Isn't there a verse that tells us the types of thoughts to engage in? In Philippians. Whatsoever things are true, whatsoever things are honest...*

She would focus on those things, and what was lovely and true. God's love was true. She held loveliness in her arms, didn't she? Luna. And Rose, too, as she crawled across the rug, leaving a trail of lost socks behind her.

Beatie's phone quacked her text alert, making Rose laugh. "Oh, there's Dutch. He's listening to the police chatter on his phone. He says the accident isn't on the road into town. But it is—"

A pair of headlights shone into the window. Natalie spun, recognizing Wyatt's familiar truck in the glow of the streetlamps and porch light. "He's here." *Thank You, God.*

She rushed to the front door, pulling it wide-open. The noise of rain pattering on the porch roof was louder than a drumline in her ears as she stepped onto the cold concrete in her socks.

The cab light went on as Wyatt cut the ignition. She couldn't read his expression through the rain, but it seemed like he paused when he caught sight of her standing there. Then the driver's side door opened, and Ranger rushed out to her, followed by Wyatt with his work bag.

She didn't stop Ranger to dry him off. She didn't care

about wet fur or paws. All she cared about was reaching for Wyatt's coat and half pulling him up the steps so she could wrap him in her arms. Well, arm. She still held Luna, squished between them.

"What's wrong?" He didn't let go, but his tone was worried.

She breathed in the faint remnants of this morning's aftershave clinging to his neck. "Beatie and I received severe weather alerts on our phones. There was a car accident. We didn't know where you were."

Beatie appeared at their side, hands folded like she was a diver about to part the waters. "Break it up for a second and hand me the baby. You're crushing her."

Luna wasn't complaining, but Natalie handed her over. It was time for her to stop hugging Wyatt, anyway. Things were awkward enough between them without her clinging to him like a life preserver.

She followed Beatie into the house. Rose was sitting on the hall floor with Ranger, giggling while Ranger shook off the rain. Natalie gathered Rose and smooched her round cheek. "Good thing you haven't had a bath yet."

A shrill tone carried from Wyatt's coat pocket. "That must be the alert finally reaching me. How bad was the accident? Do we know who was in it?"

"No, but I think Dutch texted Beatie with more information."

Beatie held up her phone as if to prove it. "Sounds like a downed tree caused a single-car accident. No one was hurt, but the road up the hill is blocked for now."

Relief flooded Natalie's veins. "Thank God no one was hurt, but this weather is something else. We need to keep praying for no more damage or injury."

Wyatt took Luna from Beatie, nuzzling the top of her

head with his stubbly chin. "I would've pulled over if it got too bad. But I should've texted you so you knew when to expect me. Or shared my location on my phone. Here, I'll do that now."

One-handed, he scrolled on his phone. They hadn't enabled that app feature when they were engaged. It hadn't seemed necessary back then, and it seemed far too intimate a gesture now. But he was doing this, she assumed, to give her peace of mind for the girls' sakes, so she likewise enabled the tracking feature on her phone, too.

"Maybe you kids can show me how to do that. Dutch is always wandering off in the grocery store and I never know what aisle he's in."

"It's not always that precise, but sure. We just need Dutch's phone." Natalie's heart was still thrumming a hundred beats per minute, but she felt like she was finally starting to calm down. "Beatie, if the road's closed, you can't go home. Neither can Wyatt."

He shrugged out of his coat one-handed while he kept a firm grip on Luna. "I'll call the bed-and-breakfast down the block and see if they have any vacancies."

Beatie scoffed. "There's room enough here for all of us. Don't you each sleep in a separate room when you take turns here? I can bunk on the couch."

"Sounds good to me, but I insist you take my bed," Wyatt insisted. "The sheets are clean. I'll sleep down here."

No way could his six-two frame fit on the couch, but Natalie appreciated his gallantry. "That's fine with me."

"Slumber party," Beatie said, tapping Rose on the back.

Natalie met Wyatt's gaze. "Why don't you text your folks, then, and get some dinner. Beatie and I had stroganoff. Leftovers in the fridge. I'm going to run a bath for these two."

Susanne Dietze 125

"I'll help." Beatie took Luna from Wyatt's arms.

Within ten minutes, the girls were happily splashing in the bathtub while Beatie reached for the baby shampoo. "I've got this, if you want to clean up the entrance hall. Ranger made a bit of a mess."

"Good idea. I'll be back to help you dry them off."

Natalie gathered towels and a set of sheets from the linen closet in the hallway, as well as a pillow and extra blanket from Forrest and Cady's room. She strode straight to the living room to drop them off, finding Wyatt already splayed across the couch, his lower legs and feet draping off the edge.

"Ready for bed?"

"Just testing it out." He sat up. "Here, I'll make it up. Are the towels for Beatie?"

"One for Ranger, one for the mess in the entrance hall."

"I wiped that up with a rag, but Ranger will appreciate the towel when he comes back inside. He needed out. At least the rain is lessening."

"I hope it's almost done. Every time it rains heavily like that, it sends me into a panic. I can't help it."

"I'm sorry. The weather has made me think of Forrest and Cady, too. And how much I miss them." He took one edge of the sheet from her and, together, they laid it atop the couch cushions and tucked in the edges. "I didn't mean to make you worry."

"Water under the bridge." She didn't want to talk about that. Besides, they had other important things to discuss. "What did Solomon say about the remote work?"

His face fell. "He said he needs more time to think about it."

She wanted to punch the couch cushions. "He has already had a few weeks. What are we going to tell the investigator when she comes on Monday? It won't sound good if we have no idea what the future will look like."

"It's not what I wanted, either, but we'll tell her the truth and pray it's enough. I have to trust God with the unknown. Sometimes, I think He gives us just enough light to take one step at a time. *Thy word is a lamp unto my feet, and a light unto my path.* Do you know that verse?"

"It means God's word guides us."

"Yes, but to me, the verse also implies the road can be too dark to see what's up ahead. We have to trust, step by step, even if we're moving forward in the dark."

His words melted something inside her. It would be so nice to relax into the Lord, to trust Him to work out the difficulties rather than try to force answers, no matter how badly she wanted everything settled. Part of her brain fought back, though, as if worrying could—what?

Provide answers she hadn't been able to find despite hours of running different scenarios in her head?

Or enable her to hold on to a sense of control?

Startled, she hid her face by bending to tuck the edge of the sheet into the couch. "You're right. God has this."

"Good. You need rest tonight. Church tomorrow, and then I'm going to clean the house, top to bottom, to get ready for the home visit, so you know what that means. Time to get out your dancing shoes, because I don't clean if I can't dance."

That was Wyatt, lightening the mood. She couldn't fight the smile tugging at her lips. "Not all of us clean house while jamming to disco music like you do, Wyatt."

"Disco?" He clutched his chest as if she'd mortally wounded him. "Do I look like I listen to disco?"

Brawny Wyatt in his lumberjack-style flannel? Of course not, but it was fun to tease. "Looks can be deceiving."

"Are you asking for trouble, Natalie Dalton?"

It sounded almost flirtatious.

No, it *was* flirtatious. A hundred percent.

Her brain screamed for help. This was exactly how she'd felt right before she kissed him last night. Really kissed him, forgetting all sense of time and place.

Before she came to her senses. And then crashed to earth when he told her he had a substance abuse issue.

There were some very real, very big reasons why she must keep a wide distance between them, for everyone's sakes, but he looked so handsome, so huggable, while he casually tossed the pillow in the air and caught it like a ball, green eyes sparkling, like he was about to toss the pillow at her head.

"I don't need to ask for trouble, Wyatt Teague. It seems to follow us wherever we go," she blurted. "I need to help Beatie get the girls out of the tub."

His chuckle followed her up the stairs.

"Canceled?" Wyatt couldn't have heard correctly over the noise of the coffee grinder. Monday morning, he had arrived at the house early to help with the babies and last-minute tidying. Everything was ready for the home visit except for a pot of hot coffee to go with the apple-walnut muffins Natalie had baked last night.

As the whir of the grinder fell silent, Natalie leaned against the kitchen counter, phone in her hand. "Apparently, our inspector has been out with that bad virus going around, and last night she had to rush to the ER. Pneumonia. It'll be a few more weeks before she can come back."

Wyatt winced. "That sounds awful. I pray she gets better fast. But in the meantime, I wonder where that leaves us."

"We've been rescheduled for late March."

"Seriously? But our hearing with the judge is scheduled before that."

"Not anymore." She fidgeted with the pendant around her neck. "The woman on the phone was apologetic, but she said the schedule in family court is packed. Also, things will be understaffed before Easter. It's spring break for a lot of people, including the judge's kids, so this was the best they could do."

After news like this, Wyatt wanted her to smile. "There are some positive to this situation. The house is clean. So is Ranger." The sweet smell of doggy shampoo still lingered around the Labrador. "And we have all these apple-walnut muffins to ourselves."

"True." Her lips twitched, but then she met his gaze. "Maybe it's better that she won't be here today, since your job isn't ironed out yet. This buys us more time for that to be settled, and we should have a few other things sorted out, too."

"Like what?"

"I wish I could be with the girls all the time, but things are so tenuous at Foxtail. I need to be in the office at least part-time. I'd like to look for trusted childcare options."

"Of course. All I want is for you and the girls to be happy and healthy."

"That's what I want for you, too. So, since we find ourselves with an open morning, why don't you go back to the ranch and spend some time with Beacon?"

"Are you sure?"

"Absolutely. It's good for you and Ranger. He'll probably need another bath, though."

"I'd like to go to a meeting first. There's one this morning. If that's okay with you."

"By all means, please. Thanks for telling me where you'll be." Then she shooed him. "Take a muffin to go."

The muffin was gone before he had driven halfway down the street. In a few minutes, he was at the rec center with time to spare before the meeting started. He took a seat beside Silas, who held a steaming disposable cup of coffee. "Hey."

"Hey." Silas sat up straighter. "Don't you have something with the kids this morning?"

As Ranger settled beside him, Wyatt related the need to reschedule. "Before we run out of time, are you free to ride at Manzanita on Saturday?"

"Aside from church, it'll be the highlight of my week." Silas's features lightened. "When I'm in the saddle, I don't think about myself. I focus on the horse and what's around me. Birds. Terrain. Weather. God's creation. I like taking care of the horses afterward, too, brushing them down and cleaning the saddle. It doesn't feel like labor. It feels like a…"

"A gift?"

"Yeah. Does that sound dumb?"

"Are you kidding? I wish I'd been home to ride Beacon a lot sooner. He and Ranger have been good for me."

Silas stretched his legs. "Now I understand why therapy ranches exist. Too bad there's nothing like that around here. Instead, I keep imposing on you."

"It's no imposition, man."

The meeting started and his attention turned to the speaker, but the conversation with Silas kept playing in his head.

Now I understand why therapy ranches exist.

What would it take to get something like that up and running? After the meeting, he called Alex to brainstorm as he drove back to his parents' house. He found them seated at the kitchen table, reading the daily paper while drinking coffee, their habit when the morning chores were finished. He quickly filled them in on the investigator's illness, and his mom tutted. "Such a shame, but it can't be helped, I guess. Help yourself to some coffee."

"Thanks, and then I'd like to take Beacon out for a quick ride before I go back to the girls."

His dad looked up from the crossword. "If you don't mind, check on our repairs to the south fence while you're out. It'll save me a trip."

"Sure thing." Wyatt took a long pull of the bitter brew, allowing the heat to course through him, praying for the right words. "Did you hear that Willard Thibodeaux is retiring at the end of the year? He intends to sell his property and his stock."

"No." Mom sat back, her mouth an O. "No more Happy Hooves?"

Dad shook his head. "Who would want to buy all those old mares?"

"I might."

He couldn't have shocked his parents more if he had announced he was starting a flea circus.

Dad finally shook his head. "Are you thinking of turning around to sell them at profit? Sounds risky, considering their ages. With two babies to think about, you should be saving money, not spending it."

"I don't want to sell the mares." Wyatt pushed his mug aside. "I want to look into starting a nonprofit ranch here in town. Willard's mares are gentle and well trained. They'd be good candidates for equine-assisted therapy, working with veterans, victims, people in recovery—"

"You want to switch careers from architect to wannabe

rancher and therapist?" Dad chuckled, but there was no mirth in it.

"It's not a career move. It's a way to give back. I know I'm out of my league, so I'd partner with people who know what they're doing. Until then, I'm hoping to board the mares here at Manzanita. I'd pay the going rate, of course."

Mom patted his arm. "Since you started going to church, you've been so considerate of others, but your plate is too full to add on something like this."

"And starting a business takes a lot of capital, which you don't have," Dad added.

"But you know what you do have?" His mom sounded so cheery, she might break into song. "A wonderful job and two beautiful babies."

"Speaking of those love bugs." Dad's tone was as chipper as Mom's. "It's their first Easter coming up, and your mom wants to host a big breakfast in the barn."

An outsider might think his parents were in good moods, but Wyatt knew better. This was their way of closing the conversation. Wyatt felt like a chastised ten-year-old, the way they changed the subject like that.

But he wasn't a kid anymore, or even the man he'd been one year ago.

It was high time he told them about his addiction, and it might help them understand why he wanted to contribute to an equine therapy program, but he wasn't in the right headspace. It would have to wait until he was calmer, and when they weren't as dug in when it came to avoiding a heavy topic.

He would, however, hold his ground when it came to the girls. "Thanks, but we'll be at church Easter morning."

"We'll do brunch, then." Mom rubbed her hands together. "Come over after the service."

"I'll ask Natalie if she already has plans." He stood up. "I'm going to change and ride, and I'll let you know about that fence, Dad. And I'm going to buy those horses from Willard."

"You can't board them here." Dad sounded gruff. "I don't want to encourage you to make such a poor business decision."

"Then I'll explore other options. See you later."

It took a while to calm down. Riding Beacon helped him refocus, but he wasn't fully at ease a few hours later when he drove to Forrest and Cady's. In fact, for the first time in a long time, he felt...

He wasn't sure how he felt. Naming emotions was as difficult as acknowledging he was experiencing them.

Time to get out the tool kit. First, prayer. Second, reach out to Alex. He parked in front of the house, spoke to God for a few minutes and then dialed his friend.

"You feel helpless," Alex said after listening to Wyatt. "Frustrated and hurt that your parents refuse to really hear what you're saying, deflated because their approval is based on your performance and maybe even weak, because all these emotions might make you want to escape."

Wyatt rubbed his forehead. "I'm that easy to read, huh?"

"You're a member of the human race. We all crave blessing from our parents. To be heard, seen, known and loved." Alex made a sound like he could relate. "You're a strong guy who can take care of himself, but one thing you've learned this past year is how much you need Christ's strength. It's tough, but He's got you, brother."

"I know." But he would feel better if he knew exactly how to make things work out. Was this how Natalie felt a lot of the time, needing a sense of control? If so, he better understood that her drive came from a place of pain, because she had been disappointed so much. "Thanks for listening. It helped a lot."

"That's what friends are for. Let me know what you hear from your boss. Maybe if he says no to the prefabricated cabin kits and working remotely, you should consider going into business for yourself."

"My cousin mentioned the same thing, but my dad reminded me how difficult it would be here in Goldenrod."

After disconnecting the call, Wyatt shifted to get out of the truck, but he didn't open the door. Despite what his dad had said, despite the potential risks, could he possibly start a business selling prefabricated cabin kits?

If he did, he could work from Goldenrod…but it would probably take a while to get off the ground and make a living at it. His dad was right that Wyatt had no capital, and he also wanted to buy Willard's stock.

It would be far better if he could keep the job he had, working remotely, but it was nice to know Alex thought his idea good enough that he could go solo.

Wyatt's steps were lighter as he strode up the walk. Natalie opened the door before he could knock. She had changed out of her dressy clothes and into jeans and a fuzzy cream sweater. "Welcome back. You seem like you're in a good mood."

"Despite a conflict with my parents, I am. Thanks for encouraging me to do something for myself this morning, Nat. I never feel like I can return the favor, though."

"Sorry to hear about your parents, but yes, you do that for me. I'm going to Foxtail now that you're here."

"No, I mean something rejuvenating. Like when you used to spend an hour looking around the bookstore. Why don't you grab coffee with a friend before or after your next

Bible study?" He followed her into the living room, where the girls played with chunky blocks. "Any time, really."

"Sounds nice, thanks. So, what happened with your parents?"

"I had the idea of starting up a nonprofit equine-assisted therapy ranch in town. I'm not qualified to run something like that, of course, but Willard's horses would be perfect for this type of work, and I could partner with people who know what they're doing. My parents aren't willing let me board the mares at Manzanita in the interim, though."

"That's too bad. A place like that could help a lot of people."

"Exactly. I can tell you more after I greet the girls." He set his phone and keys down on the coffee table so he could sit on the floor.

His ringtone chimed. "Whoever it is can wait." The girls were climbing him like a tree, and he wouldn't trade it for anything.

Natalie glanced at the screen. "It's Solomon, Wyatt."

Okay, maybe that one thing. This was too important to let go to voicemail. He gently removed the girls from his lap and took the phone from her.

He didn't need to relate Solomon's decision to Natalie when he ended the call. She could read it on his face.

"How could he refuse your request to work remotely, even once a week?" Anger furrowed her brow. "You finished those extra tasks for him, even though you've been on leave, which is more than enough proof that you can do your job well from here. Did he at least like the cabin kit proposal?"

"Nope." Frustration roiled in his gut. "And he informed me I'm needed in Arizona next month to personally kick off a project for a big client. Right when the cabin construction is wrapping up here."

"Oh." She looked down, fidgeting with the stack of coasters on the side table. "Well, I can handle it, but we should get that on the calendar so I can plan around it. You never used to travel before. When did that change?"

"This is a first. My career is important to me, but if Solomon is making changes to my job description that take me away from Goldenrod, it might be time to sever ties."

"We've talked about this, though. You're overqualified for any available work in town."

He didn't want to get her hopes up by sharing the germ of an idea to go into business for himself. That way she wouldn't be disappointed if it didn't work out. "I've got an idea. My family leave ends right before our appointment with the investigator, so I'll use a week of vacation so I can be here for another week, all right?"

"Sure, and then you'll move back to Irvine to work during the week, and come back here on weekends, right?" Her tone was guarded, as if she wasn't sure that's what she wanted anymore.

It definitely wasn't what he wanted to do. "I'd rather commute every day."

"But that's such a long drive, Wyatt. If you stay in Irvine during the week, you would only have to make that drive on weekends."

"I know that's what we discussed, but I hate the idea."

"You'll be exhausted."

"I'll be fine, and you need some nights to yourself midweek."

"If you're sure. We can reevaluate later, if you want."

"Sure, when we come up with a better solution. Together, with God, okay?"

"Okay. We're going to trust Him." To his surprise, she reached up and hugged him.

Some wounds could only be healed by God. He knew that. But Natalie's gentle embrace eased the stings of the day like nothing else. She was balm in his arms, peace and comfort that he didn't want to release.

Ever. There was no bliss like what he found in her nearness, her kiss.

But they were not that kind of partners, and when she pulled back, he let her go.

Chapter Nine

〜

"I don't think the house can get any cleaner, Nat."

Natalie wasn't so sure. Despite their best efforts to keep
up with housework, it was difficult with the messes two
crawling babies and a dog created just by existing. She had
been preparing for today's investigator visit since the calendar page flipped to March over two weeks ago, scrubbing,
polishing, buffing and waxing. Every surface in the house
shone, but it wasn't enough. "I just found three Cheerios, a
gross pacifier and a tuft of Ranger's fur beneath the couch."

"I don't think the investigator will be looking under the
furniture." Wyatt gave an indulgent shake of his head as
he plugged the vacuum cleaner into a wall socket. "She's
coming to evaluate the girls' well-being, not count dust
bunnies."

"I would, if I were her."

"Seriously?" His brows knit.

She scanned the living room for the umpteenth time,
looking for fingerprints and spills. "A tidy house is important."

"So are happy kids." Wyatt grinned at Rose and Luna,
safe in the playpen watching them work. "All right, girls.
Big noise. The vacuum goes *vroom!*"

The loud motor's whir didn't sound at all like *vroom*,

but the babies loved his vacuum impression, as well as the way he made silly faces at them while he pushed the cleaner over the living room rug—an act he'd invented a week or so ago to counter the fearful way the girls responded to the loud appliance.

Natalie enjoyed his vacuum show, too. She couldn't help but notice the way his thin sweater strained over the muscles of his broad back and shoulders. He shut off the vacuum and wound up the cord, and goodness—was there such a thing as a vacuum cleaner model? Because the way he hauled the vacuum in one arm to put it away in the hall closet, he could sell hundreds. Thousands. Millions. Natalie had to look away.

He returned to the room, brushing off his hands. "All done, with an hour to spare."

"Plenty of time to go over the bathrooms again."

"Plenty of time to get antsy sitting around waiting, you mean. Let's get out of the house so we don't mess it up. Burn off some energy. How about a walk in the orchard? It's been a while."

"But we're already dressed up." The girls wore floral rompers. Even Ranger was dapper in a pale blue bow tie.

"I meant to ask you, how do I look?"

"Nice." Understatement of the year, in that sweater. "You look *really* nice. I like that dress."

Do not read anything into him being polite. "Thanks. I'd hate for us to get dusty on a walk."

"We won't. But if we do, we can change when we get home. You don't even need to change shoes. Those seem nice and flat, and the orchard paths are smooth."

"All right, but you need to help me keep Ranger out of any foxtails." The weeds had sprouted up all over the orchard with the spring rains, and their barbed seed heads were potentially dangerous if they embedded in a dog's skin.

"No foxtails." He grinned, scooping the babies out of the playpen, one in each burly arm. "That's what the orchard is named for, right? Weeds?"

She saw right through Wyatt's attempts to curb the anxiety burgeoning in her. And frankly, she appreciated it. "Very funny. You know the story about the fox."

"Right after your great-grandparents settled on the property and planted apple trees, a fox made a regular habit of visiting them," he said, leading her to the front door. "For the longest time, they never saw its face, just its tail sticking out from behind a tree, but eventually, it showed its face. And your Granny Dalton named it Fred."

"Felix." She gathered her purse, Ranger's leash, and the diaper bag from the hall table. "Felix the Fox."

From the twinkle in his eye, it was clear he knew it was Felix all along. "Granny Dalton wanted to name the orchard Felix Farm, but Grampy Dalton named it after the weeds, instead."

She groaned as she locked the door behind them. "After Felix's tail, Wyatt. As you well know. Goodness, the babies will start to believe you."

"You know I'm teasing, right, duck?" he asked Rose, buckling her into the car seat.

"Moo boo," she said.

"Exactly." He winked at her.

Grinning, Natalie secured Luna, then Ranger, in the back seat and tossed Wyatt her keys. "Let's go."

After the short drive, they parked at the farm stand and loaded the babies into the stroller. After obligatory stops at the farm stand and the cabin site—which was progressing nicely—they took the path to the Granny Smith orchard.

Leaf tips emerged in flashes of green on the branches, promising blossoms soon. In time for Esme's wedding, though? All Natalie could do was pray for blooms in at least one of the orchards for the big event.

"Are you thinking about the investigator?" Wyatt pushed the stroller while she held Ranger's leash.

"No, the wedding next month. I should be focused on today, though."

"Both will turn out fine. God's got them."

Wyatt had always been an optimist, but now, with God in his life, his confidence was based on more than his personality. It was based on trusting God cared for them.

The topic was the first thing on Natalie's mind every morning. *Would she choose to trust today?*

Would she trust God, believing He had a plan for all the things that concerned her, or lean on her own understanding, as the Scripture said in Proverbs?

Trust Wyatt, when his presence made her thoughts scramble like eggs in a skillet?

Since admitting his addiction to her, he hadn't given her any reason to doubt him. As he had promised, he was transparent about his attendance at recovery meetings, and up front when he stepped out to take calls from Alex or the unnamed friend who had called him the night of their dinner at the Hollow. She would never ask the identity of that person, because it didn't matter. Now that she understood the bond they shared, she wanted nothing but healing for all of them.

He also seemed to be working hard to earn her trust, too, devoting himself to the girls, the cabin and cleaning for today's home visit.

And yet…and yet… Natalie still couldn't ignore the past. Wyatt had left once. One week from today, he would start commuting back and forth every day, a long drive, rather than staying in Irvine all week and only spending the weekends in Goldenrod.

She feared it would wear him out.

Or perhaps, once he returned to the life he'd found away from her, he might realize how much he'd missed it. What would happen then?

Would he leave the girls? Slowly at first, but steadily, until they didn't know him anymore?

No. He wasn't her father. She had to trust him. Trust God.

The longer she continued in her women's Bible study, the more she yearned to give God her troubles, doubts and fears. It seemed when she did, though, it wasn't long before she took them back. All she could do was confess her struggle and pray for God's strength as she walked with Him, one step at a time, no matter how dark the path.

"Look at that." The awe in Wyatt's voice pulled her from her thoughts. They were almost to the edge of the orchard, an unmarked boundary between the property her family had developed and acres of untouched land. It was Natalie's favorite place at Foxtail.

They stopped just beyond the last of the Granny Smith trees. There, in the gentle shadow of pines and elder trees, wild grasses waved in the meadow. To the left—the west—Golden Delicious trees grew in neat rows, and to the right, the snow-dusted peaks of the mountains pointed to the cloudless blue sky. "The beauty of this view never ceases to take my breath away."

"Nor mine." Natalie took a deep breath, savoring the sweet tinge of spring dancing in the air. "I've never understood why no one built a house here."

"It's far from the main road, I guess."

"But it wouldn't have been difficult to carve a private drive around the farm stand."

Wyatt rubbed his chin, like he was envisioning it. "Doable. Someday you can look into it."

"When the money rolls in," she said with a laugh. "There's so much good land at Foxtail that could be used to generate income, but we can't touch it until we meet the conditions of my dad's will. No expanding Thatcher's ranch. No more apple trees or other crops. No renting out the land for grazing or selling off parcels. I do not understand why my dad did this to us, binding us here and not letting us change anything."

"Someday we might comprehend Asa's intention, but for now?" Wyatt dug into the diaper bag and withdrew the babies' snack container. "Tell me how you'd build a house here. If you had the means."

"Big, wide windows and a porch for the view. A laundry room. And if it were two stories, I'd love a high entrance hall. They give a house an airy feeling." His approving grin made her stomach flip. "Hey, are you trying to distract me so I don't worry about the investigator?"

"It's not worth getting worked up about, especially when we can pray. Want to do that now?" Wyatt's easy smile soothed her nerves. So did his prayer, lifted beneath the shade of an elder tree.

This is what I want for my forever. A husband who prays.

Except Wyatt was not her husband. And this was certainly not the time to be thinking about things that confused and challenged her.

Like the way Wyatt bent to pull Luna from the stroller when they reached the car again, and how she snuggled into him. Wyatt's expression softened into one of pure contentment, and Natalie's heart melted like butter on a stack of pancakes.

Maybe it was because he was such a large man who became a teddy bear with a tiny child in his arms. Maybe it was the sweetness on his face she'd never seen until he fell in love with Rose and Luna.

Or maybe it was because she was drawn to him. Still.

She shoved the thought back to the recesses of her brain. They needed to be friends for the girls' sakes, nothing more.

She just wasn't sure where the boundary line fell anymore.

A week after the successful visit with the investigator was Wyatt's first Easter as a believer, and he couldn't stop smiling.

Granted, his photo was being taken, and he had to smile. But celebrating the resurrection held profound meaning to him, and having Natalie and the babies by his side hit something deep within, making him feel more content than he could remember.

"Say 'cheese,' you guys. No, say 'bunny'!" Sadie held her phone just so, her fingers stretching the image on her screen, while Wyatt propped Luna on his arm.

Thatcher, standing beside Sadie, smirked. "I can't hear you say 'bunny,' Wyatt."

Wyatt snorted. "Because I'm already smiling, man. Your turn next."

"No way." Thatcher waved his hands. "I'm not getting up there. Mick will, though."

"Dude." Mick rolled his eyes.

Before the girls became a permanent part of his life, Wyatt probably would have felt the same about standing in front of the pastel floral backdrop his parents had set up for their brunch party in the vacant barn at Manzanita Ranch. But now, he'd gladly embrace it. How could he resist pictures with the girls, who were beyond adorable in the dresses Cady had picked out for them months ago?

It was bittersweet, knowing Cady and Forrest should be here with Rose and Luna. Instead, he and Natalie posed with them for the photo.

Or photos, rather. Sadie seemed to be taking about a hundred.

"Did you get a good shot yet?" Natalie, pretty in a pale purple dress, shifted beside him, switching Rose from one arm to another. "Rose is getting bored."

Sadie scrolled through her phone. "Her dress is all bunched up. Can you fix it?"

Wyatt broke his pose, freeing Rose's skirt from where it was pinned by Natalie's arm. Then he bent to kiss Rose atop her fuzzy head. "Just a few more, duck."

Something pinched his ear, holding him in his half-bent-over position. Rose's grip. Gently, he tried to twist out of her hold, but she pinched harder and then shrieked in laughter. She was enjoying this. So, apparently, was Luna, who burst into giggles.

"Ow, Rosie. We need to trim your nails."

Natalie cackled. "I'm sorry, but you should see your face, Wyatt."

It was no use fighting it. Wyatt laughed, too.

Sadie rushed forward, her phone in their faces. "This is pure gold. Wait until you see these."

"I might lose an ear if we wait too much longer." But the way he was pinned in place, his face was close to Natalie's. Standing inches from her, breathing in the floral scent of her perfume, unlocked a flood of memories, of golden teenage summers when he first fell for her, hard. The nervousness he hid behind a bravado when he asked her out for the first time. The anticipation he felt when he'd proposed, and she'd accepted before all the words he had rehearsed were out of his mouth.

As much as he wished he could go back in time, he couldn't ignore the mighty works God had brought about in the past year. Since following Jesus, he'd felt a love greater than any he had ever known. A sense of peace that had nothing to do with his circumstances.

And joy in this moment, here with Natalie, Luna and Rose, despite the tinge of sadness at missing Forrest and Cady.

Once Sadie was satisfied with the photos, they stepped away from the backdrop. A crowd of fifty or so were gathered in the barn, socializing and sampling appetizers— mostly friends of his parents, but Natalie's family, too, including Dutch and Beatie. His parents broke off from their conversations, marching over.

"Howdy hey." Dad reached to take Luna from Wyatt. She didn't seem to mind, so he let her go. While Wyatt still ached that his parents didn't approve of his idea for a therapy ranch, still dreaded talking to them about his addiction for fear they would reject him—or worse, ignore that part of him—he was determined to foster their relationship.

Because I love them, Lord, and because they need You.

"Happy Easter," his mom said, opening her arms to embrace each of them.

Natalie returned her hug. "Thanks for hosting us, Jillian, Gary. It looks amazing in here."

"It does." Wyatt kissed his mom's cheek. She was a whiz at this sort of thing, crafting Easter basket centerpieces to sit atop each yellow-clothed table and adding clumps of faux grass and dyed eggs on just about every flat surface.

The air was scented with honey-baked ham and spring blooms, while conversations floated over the faint strains of a folk ballad playing on the sound system.

"Our pleasure." Jillian reached for Rose. "There's so much for us all to celebrate. The home visit with the investigator being over, and of course, we're so proud of the success of Mick's event back on Valentine's Day."

Wyatt's throat tightened. Proud of the *success of the event*, not Mick himself. Did his parents realize they spoke like that? Wyatt had never heard his parents say *I'm proud of you*. If Wyatt wanted attention or praise growing up, he had learned he had to accomplish something to get it. Having grown up in the same house, Mick surely had, too.

His cousin smiled now, though. "Thanks, Aunt Jillian. We raised a good amount of money for the shelter, and most importantly, those animals found forever homes."

"Don't you mean *fur*-ever homes?" Dad glanced up from Luna, who was patting his gray mustache.

Mom ignored the pun. "We've been thinking about your plan to commute to Irvine every day, son. It doesn't sound sustainable. Or realistic."

"I'm not looking forward to it, but I want to be in town with the girls as much as possible."

Dad bounced Luna in his arms. "Seems like you're kicking the can to avoid the inevitable. Sooner or later, you'll get sick of the commute and stay put in Irvine. Maybe you should move back to Irvine and sell Forrest and Cady's house, now, so you can get on with your lives."

Wyatt froze. "Rose and Luna *are* my life, Dad—"

His mom forced a laugh, cutting him off. "They can't sell the house, Gary. Remember, guardianship isn't formalized with the court and the house is in a trust. Besides,

Natalie can't leave Foxtail, and her place is too small for her and the girls."

"Speaking of the size of our apartments." Sadie's tone was dry. "If only we knew an architect who could design something bigger for us on Foxtail property, Natalie." She poked Wyatt in the arm. "It's not like we don't have a lot of acreage to build on."

Dove patted the table in front of Wyatt. "Ooh, if not a big house for Natalie, then maybe you can help us set up four cabins just like the one we're going to rent out, so each of us has a place of our own. Then I wouldn't have to listen to Thatcher snoring through our shared wall."

Natalie's gulp was audible, and Wyatt was confident she was thinking of Foxtail's shaky finances.

"Maybe we should eat," Wyatt suggested. Natalie mouthed *thank you* at him.

It took a few minutes to go through the food line, clamp portable infant seats to the table and secure bibs over the girls' pretty dresses. Their family members filled plates and sat with them, digging into the feast.

"Tell us more about this wedding coming up," his mom prodded Natalie. "Dove mentioned the bride hopes to get married in the middle of blossoming trees. Will it happen?"

"I think so." Natalie offered Rose a tiny bite of her scalloped potatoes. "As long as there isn't a frost, but we're prepared. I just ordered additional protective sheets for the trees."

She sounded lighthearted, but Wyatt knew her. She was concerned something would go wrong. "All your hard work is going pay off, Nat. I'm sure of it."

"It's a group effort." She gestured at her family.

"You gals, maybe, but not me." Thatcher pushed his empty plate back. "Weddings make me break out in a rash.

The only part of this plan that's remotely interesting is the cabin going up."

Natalie speared her three-bean salad. "Everything is on schedule there."

Wyatt appreciated her vote of confidence, but years of experience had taught him that something always went wrong in a project. However, he would ensure the cabin was ready in time, even if he had to finish all the work himself. In the meantime, he intended to use whatever spare time he had to find work that didn't involve a five-hour round-trip commute.

After they'd finished eating, they found themselves alone at the table. Wyatt's parents each took a baby to mingle with their guests, and while the girls seemed content, Natalie watched after them with a concerned set to her brow. "It's close to nap time. Maybe we should go home before they start fussing."

"If they do, we'll take them home." But for now, he was glad for a few minutes to talk. "I meant what I told my dad. The girls are my life now. I'm not going to get tired of commuting."

"Sure, you will." Natalie unwrapped a bright blue foil–wrapped chocolate egg set on the table for guests to munch on. "I would, if I were you. A daily commute like that sounds exhausting."

"It's worth it to me, and I want you to know I'm not going to change my mind. Okay?"

"Okay." She looked down, so he couldn't tell if she believed him or not.

Each of his parents walked with a baby, bending and holding their hands to help them "walk" past the food tables, much to the delight of the other guests. This was the sort of thing he didn't want to miss. "Luna looks a little befuddled, but Rose looks rather proud of herself."

"She sure does." Natalie smoothed out the blue foil into a shiny square. "Things are going to change a lot when the girls learn to walk. I need to go through the house for Babyproofing 2.0."

"*We* need to."

She popped the chocolate into her mouth and looked up him, her eyes wide in question.

Maybe he shouldn't have said anything, but too late now. "We. Not just you. It's a small thing, but you often speak like I'm not going to be around to help."

She swallowed. "I—I guess you're right, but you'll be busy. And you're going to Arizona for a week for work. When you get back, the cabin will close to ready. You'll have a lot on your plate."

"That doesn't mean I won't do my part."

"I didn't mean it like that. But things happen, and I want the babyproofing completed before it's necessary. That's a fundamental difference between us. You're so confident everything will work out that you don't always think about planning ahead."

"And you look for any possible pitfall and prepare for them all." His words were harsh, but his tone wasn't.

"That's what adults do, don't they? Especially when children are involved?"

"Of course, but I think there's a middle ground."

"I suppose." She reached for another mini chocolate egg. "Look at us, Wyatt. Disagreeing, in public, no less, but we're calm."

"Focused on the babies. Working through our issues like old pros. Fist bump." He offered his closed hand.

With a laugh, she gave him a soft bump.

"Guys." Dove ran to the table, her voice high-pitched with excitement. "Look."

His mom had let go of Rose's hands, and Rose stood in front of her, little brow scrunched in concentration.

"Does she want to walk?" Natalie gasped. "But she's only ten months old."

"That's our duck, though." Awe filled Wyatt's chest as he stood to cheer her. "Go, Rosie, go."

Rose lifted one dainty leg as if she were about to march. Then set it down, followed by the next leg.

"Her first steps!" Tears stung Natalie's eyes.

"I'm recording it." Sadie's phone camera was focused on the baby. "Keep going, Rosie!"

Pride, joy and awe swelled in Wyatt's chest.

And hope. Things wouldn't be easy with his commute or his upcoming business trip to Arizona, but he would be there for Natalie in every way he could.

And hopefully soon, he might even regain her trust. Permanently.

Chapter Ten

Two-and-a-half weeks after Easter, Natalie pushed the stroller behind the farm stand, her phone set on speaker. She had left the office with the babies moments before her phone rang, hardly two minutes ago, but her molars were already grinding together.

"Esme, bees are essential to the ecosystem." She kept her tone friendly so she wouldn't upset Esme or the babies. "They pollinate the trees when they move from blossom to blossom. We need them if we want a decent crop this year, and I'm not going to do anything to hurt them. If you have an allergy, maybe you can apply a repellant—"

"Ew, no, then I'd be all smelly." Esme sounded incredulous. "I'm not allergic. I just hate bugs."

Then why did you plan an outdoor wedding? "I'm not a fan of certain varieties, myself, but bees have a critical role to play in the orchard."

"Fine, but I still want some management of other insects. My friend has an apple tree, and she said the aphids make the leaves shiny. I don't want that in the photos, or spiderwebs, either. You can take care of that before the wedding, right? You have a lot of time."

Ten days, actually. While Esme droned on, Natalie flicked to the calendar app on her phone. Now that it was

April, many of the dates were filled in with important events. The cabin inspections. The wedding. The hearing at family court a few days after that. And this week, she had noted Wyatt's Arizona trip with the letters *W. AZ*.

The number of items on her to-do list was overwhelming, but God was with her.

When Esme finished her requests, Natalie ended the call, startled to see Dove watching off to the side, her red Foxtail apron speckled with flour. "Is Esme changing things up again?"

"Nothing we can't handle." Not if they wanted to book more weddings at Foxtail. They needed a good review from Esme and her lifestyle-blogger mother. "I just have to say no in a nice way."

"Better you than me. I'm too blunt." Dove greeted the babies, who responded with happy coos. "How about I take the girls on their walk and you can have a break, Nat? You could use one, with Wyatt gone all week."

"Sure, but I'm not taking a walk. I'm on my way to meet Dutch and Silas in the Gravenstein orchard. Something failed in the new irrigation system."

Dove winced as she took the stroller from Natalie. "Let's hope the problem isn't too expensive."

"Agreed, but it's better to ensure everything is done correctly so we don't pay the price later."

The farm stand's rear door opened, and Sadie stepped out, tape measure in hand. "Fancy seeing you all here. What's up?"

Natalie smiled at her sister. "Dove is taking the girls on a walk. I'm meeting Dutch and Silas in the Gravenstein orchard. You?"

"Esme sent me an email. She wants a wedding arch."

Natalie's pulse quickened. "We don't have an arch."

"I told her I'd look into it. Maybe Dutch can help me make a simple one. She also wants me to adjust the heights of some of the flower arrangements so they come right to the height of the lowest branches of the trees behind the arch, so I'm going to take some measurements."

"Wow, Esme's been busy today." Dove rolled her eyes. "She just got off the phone with Nat."

"She requested no insects at the ceremony," Natalie said.

Dove gaped, then burst into laughter. "Okay, I need details, so I'm going with you to the Gravensteins."

"Me too. I'll measure on the way back." Sadie's eyes crinkled with mirth as they started walking. "She really asked for no insects? What did you tell her?"

"I informed her of the value of bees to the ecosystem. If there's any aphid honeydew on the day of the wedding, though, I'll ask Dutch to hose it off. This experience has been frustrating for all of us, but let's remember why we're doing this."

"For Foxtail!" Dove pumped her fist in the air.

"Yi-yit!" Rose yelled, as if she were contributing to the cheer.

Sadie gasped. "Did she say Wyatt? Is that her first word?"

"Maybe," Natalie conceded. Rose could be speaking baby babble, but it sounded close enough to *Wyatt* that she would jot it down in Rose's baby book when she got home. And she would text Wyatt about it later. He would crow if he were here.

Sadie bent down to the stroller. "Are you asking for Wyatt, Rosie? He'll be back this weekend. Hey, why are you wriggling like that? Are you trying to get out from your seat belt?"

"She wants to walk. Everywhere, all the time. Even when she isn't looking where she's going." Her little legs often took her in a different direction than she was looking. She would get the hang of it soon, but for now?

Good thing she and Wyatt had finished babyproofing the house, just as he had promised. Now, the sharp edges of the coffee table were covered in foam guard cushions, the doorknobs were covered so only adult hands could twist them and nonslip pads had been shimmied beneath all the rugs in the house.

Rose squawk's grew more insistent, so Natalie stopped the stroller and came around the side to unbuckle her. "You have to hold a hand if you want to walk, Rose."

"I volunteer." Sadie scooped Rose out and set the baby on her feet. Luna relaxed back into her seat, perfectly content to ride while Natalie pushed the stroller.

Dove's shoulder nudged Natalie. "How is ol' Yi-yit doing in Arizona, anyway?"

"Busy. Oh—Sadie, try to keep her out of the weeds."

"Sorry." Sadie guided her back onto the path. "She's okay, though."

Sadie sounded like Wyatt, not looking ahead for potential dangers, and Natalie would tell her what she told him. "Those foxtails can poke through her romper and stick into her skin—"

"Sorry," Sadie repeated. "You were saying, about Wyatt?"

Natalie rubbed her forehead. "He works all day and dines with the client every night. But in good news, he and Willard Thibodeaux have come to an agreement on a price for the mares for a therapy ranch. Wyatt just needs somewhere to stable them."

"Sounds like Wyatt is definitely moving back to Goldenrod."

"Maybe."

"What do you mean, maybe? He's got a pet project in

the works for a therapy ranch in town. And he's open to finding work here, right?"

"Yes, but…" She huffed out a breath. "Working here means giving up his dream job and taking on something unsatisfying. He will grow resentful and then he might leave again."

Dove shook her head. "Remember when Dad died? The three of us and Thatcher dropped everything to move back to Foxtail. We all grumble about Dad's will from time to time, but when it comes down to it, we all wanted to honor Dad and one another, so we don't all lose our individual shares of the inheritance. I don't care so much for me, because I can work anywhere, but can you imagine if Thatcher lost the ranch? He'd be miserable."

"We all love this land," Sadie added. "None of us want to see it parceled off at auction. Anyway, that's what Wyatt is doing. He will gladly give up his 'dream job' to be here for the girls. And for you."

"Not for me." Natalie's stomach clenched. "Please don't assume he wants to be here for me."

"You guys are getting along really well. At least, it looks that way to us. And he sure has stepped up." Sadie's hopeful tone pierced Natalie's heart. "Don't you think he deserves another chance? Maybe you could eventually knit back together again."

Natalie stared at the ground. "I won't lie and say I feel nothing for him, but what if we got back together and it didn't work out? I don't want to get hurt again. Or for the babies to get hurt, the way we were every time Dad took off."

"Dad really did a number on us, didn't he?" Sadie let out a long sigh. "I'm not sure Dove and I were affected quite the same way you were, because we were too young. I don't even remember Dad living with us. All the things that followed, sure. The times he'd forget to call on our birthdays. The fights he and Mom had over the phone. But you have more trauma from the early days, Nat. It's no wonder you don't trust Wyatt to stay. But you two are building a totally different foundation than the one our parents had in their relationship. I know he left before, but... I don't think Wyatt's like that."

Rose yelped.

Sadie looked at Natalie. "She doesn't want to hold my hand anymore. Should I let her go?"

There were fewer weeds here, and the path was wider. "I guess. Just watch her so she doesn't veer into trouble."

Sadie released Rose's hand. Rose toddled forward, enjoying simply putting one foot in front of the other. They were well into the Cripps Pink orchard, surrounded by rows of trees spaced to accommodate their wide canopies. Wild grasses sprouted around the trunks, which gave Natalie hope the trees would bloom before the wedding. It also indicated the irrigation system was working fine here, which reminded Natalie why she was in the orchard to begin with. "Thanks for talking. I should go meet Dutch and Silas—"

"Goodness, look at that." Sadie's voice was hushed in awe. "The farm might have been named in honor of the foxes here, but I haven't seen one in a while."

Sure enough, a sleek gray fox pattered across their path some twenty yards ahead. Although the critters were nocturnal, it wasn't unheard of for them to be out in daylight, especially in spring when they had kits to feed. If this one had babies in a den nearby, it could grow alarmed easily.

Time to pick up Rose. Natalie reached for her, but the baby giggled and broke into a clumsy run.

Natalie lunged. She didn't see the mud until she was already slipping. She flung out her arms to brace for her fall, landing hard on her palms before rolling onto her backside.

A river of pain sluiced through her right arm. "Grab Rose."

"I've already got her." Sadie, holding the baby, squatted beside Natalie. "Are you hurt?"

"I'll be okay." Natalie sat up, cradling her arm. "I just need a minute."

Dove shook her head. "What you need is an X-ray."

"It's not broken." Natalie winced. "I don't have time for it to be broken."

Dove bit her lip. Sadie let out a long breath.

Natalie groaned. "I know, it's broken."

"Let's go to the ER." Dove pulled out her phone.

"I'll drive her. You take the babies?" Sadie murmured to Dove.

"Sure," Dove murmured back, buckling Rose back into the stroller. "I'll let Dutch know you can't meet him. I'll call Wyatt, too."

"Don't tell Wyatt, okay?" Natalie didn't need him.

Want him? Yes, despite herself. Wanted him to kiss her brow and tell her everything would be all right—the wedding and the orchard and the long, uncertain future they would share raising the girls.

But she didn't *need* him. And she didn't want to lean on him, so that no matter how many business trips he took or weeks he spent away from her and the girls, so that if he truly left her, she would survive.

She did a fair job of convincing herself of it, too, through the ER visit and a long, uncomfortable night, until the next morning. Sadie was washing breakfast dishes and the babies were playing with pots and pans on the kitchen floor when a knock pounded on the front door. Before Natalie could get down the hall to answer it, the scrape of a key in the lock mechanism sounded, and the door flung wide.

Wyatt's form filled the doorway. "Nat, what are you doing out of bed?"

The gruff tone to his voice made her breath catch.

But before she could say a single word, he hoisted her off her feet, into his arms.

"Put me down." Natalie's demand reverberated in Wyatt's ear.

"I intend to." Shaking the ringing sensation from his ear, he marched into the living room and lowered her onto the couch, gently propping her back against the cushions so he wouldn't jar her right arm, hanging across her chest in a black sling. "What do you need? Tylenol? Crackers? A magazine?"

"How about answers? You're supposed to be in Arizona."

That answer seemed obvious. "I left a day early."

"Ahem." Sadie appeared in the doorway, eyes wide with unabashed curiosity. "The girls and I are going to Foxtail now. We will be back for lunch and naps."

Natalie pushed herself up one-handed, then grimaced. "But—"

"Bye." Sadie waved, stepping away.

"Bye." As much as Wyatt wanted to see Rose and Luna, he appreciated Sadie's gesture so he and Natalie could have some time alone.

"Who told you? About this, I mean?" Natalie lifted her sling.

"Beatie." He propped himself on the edge of the couch, sitting sideways so he could face her. "I would have preferred to hear it from you, though."

"I didn't want you to cut your trip short. This is nothing big."

"It is to the rest of us." Wyatt let his gaze examine every square inch of her arm, down to her unpolished fingernails. "How bad is it?"

"Proximal radius fracture. The doctor called it FOOSH: falling on outstretched hand. It should be better in six weeks."

Wyatt refrained from taking her back into his arms and not letting go. Instead, he rubbed his jaw, the thick stubble reminding him he hadn't shaved since yesterday. After Beatie's text late last night, he had booked the first flight home. "You must be in terrible pain."

"It's manageable, sort of."

"That's still more pain than I want you to be in. And you must be frustrated. Six weeks is a long time without the use of your dominant hand. No writing, texting—"

"Or lifting anything heavier than a teacup."

Despite himself, his gaze fell to her mouth. "If you need any teacups elevated to your lips, I'm at your service."

Her eyes rolled. "I think I'll manage."

He moved to the wing back before he did something stupid, like kiss her. "I mean it, though. I'm here to help."

"Do you have more vacation days that I don't know about?" Her brow quirked.

"I do not. But the next ten days are critical to Foxtail Farm, and you're down for the count."

She flung her hale arm over her eyes. "Please don't."

"Don't what?"

"Make me want to rely on you. You have commitments elsewhere. You should fly back to Arizona. Or go in to work. If you leave now, you can make it by lunch."

"I'm where I want to be, and if Solomon has a problem

with it, well, I don't want to keep working in Irvine, anyway."

"You can't quit unless you find something else here." Her mouth twisted in annoyance.

Yes, but how could he leave her when she was injured? Besides, he had news. Not the great kind. "On a different note... I heard from one of the inspectors this morning. The cabin isn't going to be ready as fast as I thought it would."

Her arm fell away from her face. "Are you serious?"

"It *will* be ready before the wedding. Just not as early as I anticipated. I'm sorry. The matter will be addressed before the inspector returns next week."

"Is this something I can handle, or do you need to be here?"

"A licensed architect needs to be here, and the only time I could get an appointment is for next Wednesday. I can't get out of a meeting that day in Irvine, so I asked Alex if he was interested in taking over here."

"Your friend?" Her brow furrowed. "He would drive all the way out here? How much does he charge?"

"Nothing. This is friendship, not business."

Well, that wasn't completely accurate. After Wyatt called him, Alex had decided to take next week off to visit Goldenrod. He was coming as a friend, but he also wanted to get a good look at the cabin.

Because this trip to Arizona had confirmed something to Wyatt. He wanted to be here, full-time. As his own boss, designing prefabricated cabin kits.

And Alex was interested in partnering with him.

But Wyatt didn't want to get Natalie's hopes up about a venture that might not happen, especially if Alex didn't like what he saw, so he would wait to say anything.

Lord, Your will be done. He prayed it over and over, although he also hoped this path was God's will. The idea of going into business for himself, doing something he loved, here, where his loved ones were? It filled him with excitement.

"That's really nice of Alex." Natalie's voice held a hopeful tinge. "When can I schedule the furniture delivery, do you think? Next Thursday is the last possible day."

"Thursday is safest." He stood. "Don't worry about the cabin. It will be finished in time for the wedding, and I will do everything I can to ensure you have time and space to rest and work. When I can't care for the girls myself, I'll set up childcare. Oh, and Beatie mentioned that the bride wants a wedding arch. I'll take care of that, too."

"You don't have time—"

"It's a simple job. I'll set up the girls in a playpen while I work."

"Thank you, Wyatt. This truly helps."

Her lips might be off-limits, but he bent over the couch and kissed her hairline, breathing deeply. No shampoo or cosmetic smell, only the fragrance he'd never been able to define beyond the perfume of her. Warmth, wheat and lavender, intoxicating and perfect. "You gave me quite a scare, you know."

"You've never been scared of anything."

If she only knew.

The next few days passed in a blur of little sleep, countless phone calls over Bluetooth while he commuted and far less time with Rose and Luna than he wished. He worked out a childcare schedule, finding volunteers, including his mom, two of her knitting club friends and one of the teenagers employed at the farm stand.

And in the meantime, the world fully entered spring. The foothills along his commute blossomed with patches of mountain lilac, grape soda lupine, paintbrush, yarrow and goldenrod. The apple trees greened, the days grew longer and the breezes off the mountaintops no longer felt brisk.

Alex arrived on Saturday, and they shared dinner with Natalie's family at the farmhouse. While Wyatt was glad everyone seemed to like his friend, he wished he had time alone with Natalie. She looked tired, and her arm probably bothered her more than she let on.

Lord, all I want is to lift the weight from her shoulders. But how?

Wednesday was the cabin's inspection day, and midday, his phone buzzed with a message from Alex.

Wyatt responded, then texted Natalie.

Passed inspection! Can we get our first look at the cabin together, tonight?

Her reply was quick.

Your mom is feeding the girls dinner so I can work late. Meet me at Foxtail when you arrive in town.

Wyatt praised God the whole drive back to Goldenrod. He pulled into Foxtail Farm around seven and found Natalie in the office, squinting at her computer screen. She was beautiful as ever, but she looked weary after a long day.

He rapped his knuckles against the door. "Hey, ready to go?"

She rubbed her eyes. "Yes, I can't wait to see it."

She led the way around the farm stand to the path, past the picnic tables and fire pit, into the circle of cedars where the cottage once stood. "Maybe I can start stocking the kitchen tonight, since you'll have the girls. I'd like to get a lot done so that when the furniture arrives in the morning, it will be pretty much ready to go."

"I canceled the furniture appointment," Wyatt said.

"Why would you— Oh, my." She stumbled to a stop, her left hand covering her mouth.

Their family and friends bustled about the completed cabin, a two-story edifice of eastern white pine logs. Thatcher and Mick worked shovels into the soil in front of the cabin, deep enough to plant the rosebushes that waited on the path. Wyatt's dad pushed a dolly laden with boxes up the accessibility ramp, while Dutch swept the shallow porch, working around Beatie, who was adjusting a pair of rustic-style rocking chairs.

"You arranged all this?"

"I hope it's a pleasant surprise," he said as Ranger dashed from the open cabin door out toward them. "Beauty from ashes. Or from wood chips?"

"I thought I would have to do all this work tomorrow." She bent to pat Ranger, gaze still on the cabin. "I thought—"

"You're not alone, Natalie. You don't have to do it all yourself."

"Thank you." She leaned into him, resting her head against his chest. It was all he could do not to kiss her, but for now, he wrapped her in his arms.

Thanks, Lord. You and our friends helped us get here today, and I pray this dwelling will be a blessing to all who visit it. And please bless Natalie, too, as she strives to keep Foxtail running.

"Knock it off, you two. Time for hugging later." Beatie beckoned them forward.

Natalie laughed, breaking away to move toward the cabin.

Thatcher gave Ranger a good rubdown while Natalie

hugged each of their loved ones, gently protecting her right arm. "Thank you, all."

"You're welcome." Thatcher gestured with the shovel. "But you haven't seen anything yet. Go inside."

She raced up the porch steps into the cabin's main room. Every stick of furniture—delivered this morning without Natalie's knowledge while she worked—had been placed according to her wishes. Craftsman-style lamps, candlesticks on the mantel of the stone fireplace and a deep green rug added the perfect touches to the open floor plan.

Straight ahead in the kitchen, Dove was unloading clean silverware into a drawer and Alex, his red hair flopping over his brow, unpacked mugs from a box on the floor.

"Surprise," Dove called. "Before you ask, Rose and Luna are at the house with Sadie. She'll put them to bed if you're not back in time."

"Dishes coming through." Wyatt's dad carried one of the boxes he had maneuvered with the dolly.

Natalie wiped a tear. "You have all worked so hard."

"Many hands make light work." His dad set the box on the kitchen table and started back toward the door. "Jillian is upstairs, making the beds in the loft."

"Oh, I want to help her. I'll peek into the downstairs bed and bath when I'm done." Natalie bounded up the stairs.

Dove closed the silverware drawer. "This is so fun."

Wyatt opened the box of dishes and began to unload the contents into a cupboard. "You guys are the best."

"So is this cabin." Alex filled the water reservoir for the per-cup coffee maker. "The answer is yes, by the way. I want in. I think a lot of people will want your—our—cabin kits, partner."

"You want in?" Natalie's voice behind him made him stiffen.

"I thought you went upstairs," Wyatt noted.

"Jillian's on the phone. I didn't want to intrude so I came back down. What are you guys talking about? Are you starting a business?"

Wyatt lamented not warning Alex to keep things quiet so Natalie could hear it from him first. Too late now. "Alex and I are discussing the possibility of designing and selling prefabricated cabin kits. I could stay in Goldenrod full-time."

"It sounds wonderful." Her smile didn't look quite natural, though. Was she worried about the amount of time it could take him away from Rose and Luna?

"Nothing will happen for a while. It's the same issue I'm experiencing with the therapy ranch—ideas are great, but they need time to get off the ground."

"Not if we get a loan," Alex noted.

"I hope it becomes a reality soon. You're obviously great at this, and you'll have plenty of customers." Her gaze shifted to encompass the group. "Have you eaten? I'd love to order pizza for everyone."

"Sounds fantastic." Alex rubbed his lean stomach.

Natalie dug out her phone. "I'll step outside and call Pietro's."

Wyatt followed her out to the wraparound porch, shutting the door behind him. "Wait, Nat."

"What's up?" Her attention was fixed on her phone.

"Can we talk about my business idea?"

"It sounds like more than an idea if you've been discussing it with Alex."

"There's been so much going on, with your arm and the wedding, and I couldn't stand the thought of giving you one more thing to worry about."

"How long has this been going on?"

"Since my last day in Arizona. I talked to Alex, and he

was interested enough to come here this week and see the potential for himself. There's a lot to consider, though. I can't quit my job and start a business without causing financial strain, and I refuse to do that. Alex thinks a loan will do the trick, but first I'll have to spend weekends and evenings creating a business plan. You might worry that I'll be too busy for Rose and Luna. It's a lot to consider, and I didn't know if Alex was interested or not. I wanted to eliminate as much uncertainty as possible before I dumped all this on you."

"Maybe you thought you were protecting me, but really, you were leaving me out." She set her phone on the porch railing. "I thought we had decided not to do that anymore."

"You're right. I'm sorry. I made a poor decision. I hope you can see that I made it out of care, though. Not malice."

"Wyatt—"

"I care about you, Natalie. You and the girls, you're everything to me." Now that he'd started, he couldn't stop. "Do you care about me, Natalie?"

"Of course I do."

He waited for a *but*. Or an *as a friend*.

Thankfully, neither came. But she didn't elaborate, either.

He had to make her understand that all he wanted was for her to be well, happy. Pleased with him and the life they were forging with the babies. "When the guardianship started, we decided to build our little family, unconventional as it is, on the Lord. And we also wanted to be friends again—"

"Friends don't hide things from each other. I shouldn't be the last to know if something's going on in your life. Just so we're clear, is there anything else you're not telling me?"

Yes, there was.

Like how he wanted to kiss her again, right now.

But she wouldn't want to hear that. Yet.

Maybe ever.

He shook his head.

"Okay." She lifted her phone. "Then I should order those pizzas."

Wyatt stepped back inside the cabin, his heart pounding hard. So hard that Ranger must have sensed it, because the dog was at his side in a flash. Wyatt leaned down to scratch Ranger behind the ears, grateful for the opportunity to gather his thoughts before talking to Alex and Dove again.

He didn't just want to kiss Natalie, did he? He didn't just want a smooth and amiable future co-parenting with her. He wanted more. A real family with her and the girls.

He was falling in love with her. Again.

Lord, help me. What was he supposed to do with that?

Chapter Eleven

Natalie's every prayer for the day of the wedding had been answered, in abundance. The sky was bright blue, and the late afternoon's warmth was tempered by a gentle breeze that occasionally loosened a pink-white petal from one of the blossoming Gravenstein trees, sending it airborne like nature's confetti.

The new blossoms were gorgeous, abundant, perfect. And the smell. Oh, the smell. The flowering trees perfumed the air with their sweet, honey-like scent.

Natalie shut her eyes for a moment, inhaling deeply. *How do I thank You enough for the beauty of Your creation, Lord? For the stunning vision of the blossoming apple trees? For the faint buzz of bees and the birdsong in the air? You're amazing, Lord.*

Everything was ready for the four o'clock ceremony. Earlier today, Thatcher and Wyatt had set up the wedding arch Wyatt crafted, a simple but elegant piece that folded down for easy storage, so Foxtail could use it again. Sadie's handiwork of greenery, white and pink flowers, and clusters of apple blossoms—cuttings made with Dutch's permission from wayward branches in need of pruning anyway—transformed the arch into a beautiful canopy, beneath which the couple would exchange their vows.

Smiling guests oohed and ahhed at their surroundings as they took their seats in rows of white folding chairs. A Celtic trio off to the side played a lovely, lilting piece, and at the edge of the orchard, several steps behind Natalie, caterers had set up a large white tent for the reception.

Beatie and Dutch sidled alongside Natalie, where she stood behind the last row of chairs. "It's simply beautiful." Beatie rubbed a circle on Natalie's back. "You did amazing work."

"Not me." She gestured to her arm.

"You know what I mean."

"I do, and my answer stands. Everyone pitched in."

"There's a limit to my help. I hosed some aphids off leaves earlier for the bossy bride, but I left the bees well enough alone," Dutch said from the corner of his mouth.

Natalie bit back a laugh. "Perfect, Dutch. Thank you."

Gratitude swelled in her heart. She had fretted about pulling off the wedding, even before she broke her arm, but in the end, it was the work of others that had made this what it needed to be. The cabin wouldn't have been finished without Wyatt's long hours on the project, Alex's guidance and efforts while Wyatt was away, or the staging and decorating done by loved ones.

Nor would the wedding have been a success if Silas and Thatcher hadn't set up the chairs, unfurled the white runner down the aisle and set up signs directing guests, or if her sisters hadn't done their parts and more. Or if Wyatt hadn't encouraged her, assuring her over and over that this would work out.

I care about you, Natalie. You and the girls, you're everything to me. When he'd spoken those words the other night, her belly filled with butterflies.

And doubt. She couldn't shake the feeling there was something he wasn't telling her.

"Where's Wyatt? I thought he might still be around to watch this shindig." Beatie's question startled Natalie. Was it obvious she was thinking of him?

"He took the babies to Manzanita Ranch. Jillian is watching them while he works on a business plan for the cabin kits."

Dutch hooked his thumbs in the belt loops of his jeans. "He's a hard worker, that Wyatt. Starting a business so he can stay in town, all while working full-time out of town, plus doing his part for the girls."

"And for you." Beatie wrapped an arm around Natalie's shoulders. "After everything you two went through, it has warmed our hearts to watch him strive to make things work with you, fifty-fifty."

"I don't like that phrase, fifty-fifty." Dutch scratched at one of his long gray sideburns. "Life isn't the sort of thing you can split evenly, like an apple pie. Sure, two partners can divide labors equally, but our marriage has required all of my heart, all my effort, not half of it. I can't imagine parenthood is any different."

Beatie's arm fell from Natalie to reach for her husband's hand. "You're the smartest, handsomest man I ever met, Dutch Underhill."

"Natalie?" Sadie appeared, brows raised in a look of expectation. "After a few attempts, Esme is finally happy with the blossoms in her hairpiece, so we can start the wedding."

Natalie glanced at her watch. "Right on schedule. I'll inform the officiant. Can you signal the musicians?"

"Got it."

A few minutes later, the tall, blonde bride strode up the white runner on her father's arm, resplendent in her silk gown, smiling at her handsome groom, who waited for her in front of the blossoming trees.

As Natalie watched the couple recite their vows, it was impossible not to think of her own wedding to Wyatt—the one that had never happened. She had planned for it, though. Tried on gowns with her mom, chosen the palest of seafoam greens for the bridesmaids' dresses and started a gift registry.

All the trappings of a wedding, but none of the substance for a marriage. No couples' counseling, no deep discussion of their differences and certainly no foundation built on God.

Granted, there was a lot going on back then. Dad had died, leaving Foxtail in a mess. And Wyatt had injured his back...

It still rankled that she hadn't noticed his struggle a year ago. Maybe that was why she watched him so closely now. She still feared he might leave someday when things got hard. And wondered if he would hide things from her again, despite the talks they had about it. She understood why he hadn't told her about his plan to start a cabin kit business, but when she'd asked him if there was anything else she needed to know, her gut had screamed that he was hiding something more from her.

My gut is worth listening to, but it's not my compass, Lord. You are. Please guide me to Your truth and a place of trust. A place of acceptance.

A place where she and Wyatt could care about one another. *Care*—the word he'd used the other night at the cabin. What did he mean by it?

For the umpteenth time, she forced herself to stop analyzing his words, dwelling on them as if she were a teenager. Especially since he had been so distant since that night.

Busy, she amended. But it sure felt distant, even though he was working on the wedding arch or his new business plan when he wasn't caring for the girls—all commendable, helpful things. He had hardly spoken to Natalie the past few days, though, much less looked her in the eye.

She missed him. It was impossible to ignore the memory of curling against his chest when she saw the completed cabin for the first time. He was so huggable. So kissable.

And so, so confusing. Maybe he regretted telling her how much he cared about her, fearing she'd gotten the wrong impression.

Or maybe he was so stressed by the amount of work on his plate and his relationship with her that he was struggling with his sobriety. Maybe he wasn't working, but sneaking off to—

No. Wyatt was firm in his convictions. He had resources to help him. Her suspicious mind needed to knock it off.

As the wedding continued, Natalie's stomach pinched with yearning. Jealousy. Grief over what she and Wyatt had once had. Did she want that closeness again? She felt so drawn to him still. Always. Was it the past or the present influencing her?

"You may kiss the bride." The officiant's proclamation drew smiles to every face but Natalie's. The happy couple shared a sweet kiss and then recessed down the aisle hand in hand, grinning at their guests.

Natalie hurried to the tent, where Dove's three-tiered cake decorated with sugar blossoms sat on a round table. It looked like it could be featured in a bridal magazine, just like the low floral arrangements Sadie had crafted for each tabletop. Her sisters were artists, and they hadn't let her down.

No one had. Not even Wyatt.

Why was every line of thought returning to Wyatt today? She had set rules in place to protect herself from being hurt again. But what if he really wasn't leaving, not now or in five, ten, fifteen years? He had proven his intentions by trying to make a living here in town. Maybe the rules she'd crafted as armor around her heart were no longer necessary.

They loved one another once. The wedding reminded her how strong their feelings had once been.

She wasn't sure those feelings would ever die.

Could she and Wyatt move in a new direction, with the girls?

There was only one way to find out.

As soon as the bride and groom were finished with their photos, she pulled out her phone and texted her sisters.

If you need me, I'll be at Manzanita Ranch.

Wyatt flipped open the cap of his water bottle, the action borne out of anxiety rather than thirst. Sitting on the rough benches he had crafted years ago, beneath the shade of a thick-trunked oak in the ranch's south field where Beacon grazed, he realized this wasn't the ideal place to inform his parents of his addiction.

He had gone to Manzanita Ranch today to work on his business plan while his mom watched the girls. Nothing more. But then Mom had suggested they take the babies out in the stroller and then thought they might enjoy stretching out on a blanket in the shade. Rose and Luna now played and babbled, Ranger resting beside them, head on his front paws.

Wyatt would not have picked this moment, but the urge

to talk to his parents, really talk to them, welled up inside him, strong and demanding.

And, notably, so did peace.

Is this from You, Lord? Mom and Dad never raise their voices, but they won't like what I have to say. I would hate for them to grow heated in Rose and Luna's hearing.

Then Ranger trotted from his spot by the girls to sit by Wyatt's side, as if he knew Wyatt might need his comfort. Wyatt snapped his water bottle shut and prayed for the right words.

Before he could start, Mom looked up from watching Luna smack on a teething ring. "I haven't heard anything more about Happy Hooves going up for sale. Did Willard ever find a buyer for his land and mares?"

A perfect segue.

"As I mentioned before, I'm buying them as soon as I find a place to board them. I'm going about it backward, I know, literally putting the cart before the horse—except I'm putting the horse before the nonprofit. They're too perfect for a therapy ranch to pass up, though, and there's nothing like it in our area." He took a deep breath. "It's important to me, because I'm—"

"You've got a big heart, son." Dad cut him off. "But maybe you should leave that sort of thing to people who know what they're doing, unless you're in it for the tax write-off."

Wyatt almost laughed. Not because it was funny, but because his father's response was so typical. And so far from Wyatt's heart.

Wyatt glanced at Rose and Luna, grateful they were thoroughly occupied with their toys. "It's important to me because I'm an addict."

His parents froze, hardly seeming to breathe.

He briefly described the events of the past year, not as detailed an explanation as he had given Natalie, but enough. "Ranger has been a huge blessing to me, and so has Beacon. I want to help others experience the sort of peace I've found when I'm around these special animals."

"Like I told you earlier, I don't have room to board six mares and still have space for my regular customers." Dad didn't look at him.

That was the first thing his dad wanted to say to him? Wyatt ignored the ball of hurt solidifying in his stomach. "I didn't expect you to, after our earlier discussion. Truly. I just wanted to inform you why this is so important to me, and apologize for disappointing you."

"None of us are perfect." Mom reached over to pat his knee. "It can't have been easy to go through all that, but you're my strong boy, and now it's all in the past."

"It's also my present and future, Mom. Every day of my life I will have to choose whether to stay on the right path." He glanced at the girls, now on their hands and knees by the stroller, babbling as they investigated the wheels and nooks. "I don't ever want to let down Rose and Luna."

"That's great, son." Dad's smile was strained. "Keep up the good work. Say, Jillie, is it getting close to suppertime?"

Wyatt rubbed his forehead, unsurprised by his parents' responses, yet dissatisfied. They never tolerated talk of anything emotional or difficult for long, so he hadn't expected them to fully engage, but how could he not have wished for something more from them?

We're never disappointed in you, son. Your actions, sometimes, maybe, but you? We love you. We support you.

He would probably never hear those words from his parents.

Nevertheless, he felt peace. Accepted by God, even if his

parents wouldn't—couldn't—give him the sense of blessing he craved. God was healing him, and in the meantime, he would continue to pray for his family.

His parents discussed dinner, and the sweet sounds of babbling continued. One little babble, anyway. Not two.

He looked up. His heart stopped.

"Where's Luna?"

Natalie pulled into the lot by the Teague family stable. Before she'd left Foxtail, she had checked the friend locator app on her phone and seen the circle representing Wyatt in this location. Was he riding Beacon? Taking the girls for a walk?

As eager as she was to see Rose and Luna, she wouldn't mind catching Wyatt alone.

A peek into the stable revealed neither horses nor humans. The horses must be grazing, but where was Wyatt? She exited again, taking the path that rounded the barn, and stumbled to a stop as she almost collided with someone coming from the opposite direction.

Someone tall and broad. She wouldn't have minded literally running into him at all, if it meant she would be caught in his arms.

"Sorry, Wyatt." Her heart pattered hard and fast beneath her sling. "I almost walked right into you."

"Everything okay with the wedding? I didn't think it was over for a while." The gruff edge to his voice surprised her. So did the flush staining his neck and cheeks. She must have startled him as much as he'd startled her.

"The reception is in full swing, but I wanted to see you, and it couldn't wait." She shut her eyes a moment. "I realized something during the ceremony. All this time, with you, with us? I took my fears and made them into self-fulfilling prophecies so I wouldn't get hurt. Like if I knew something was coming, it couldn't blindside me."

The breath he took was shaky. "Wow, Nat, that's huge."

"I hoped we could talk about it."

"Yeah…sure."

Natalie's breath lodged in her chest. Something wasn't right. His tone was flat, his frame was tense and his gaze darted away from her. Like he felt antsy. Guilty, even. His hands shook at his sides. Trembled.

Had he… Oh, no. He had, hadn't he?

Her heart broke along the fault lines she had thought were healed over.

Addiction was a disease, she knew that. And she was not indifferent to his struggles, but he had promised her. Told her up and down she could count on him.

Not like this, she couldn't. "Since the girls aren't with you, I assume they're safe in the house with your parents. I'm just glad they aren't seeing you like this. Has this been going on long? Or is today the first time you've slipped up?"

His jaw dropped. "What are you talking about?"

"All this time, I thought you came here to ride Beacon, or work, or help your family…but it's obvious you've been sneaking off alone to—to take painkillers again."

"Why would you say that?" His tone wasn't just angry. He sounded hurt. "I told you I would never touch anything again, and with God's strength, I haven't. I won't. Why would you accuse me? Have you been waiting for me to fail?"

Yes, she had, she knew that now. Fail her in one way or another. But clearly she had been wise to be on her guard with him, after all. "You said you wouldn't lie to me."

"I am not lying. I am not under the influence of any substance, Nat."

"You're shaking. Red-faced. You won't look me in the eye."

Although now that he did, she could see his eyes were clear, bright. "I'm full of adrenaline, shaken up."

Further accusations died on her tongue and doom swirled in her stomach. If he was full of adrenaline, not something illicit, it was because something had happened to send him into fight-or-flight mode. Something bad. "What happened?"

He looked skyward, as if he hated to speak the words. "Mom, Dad and I took the stroller out to the south pasture. Then the girls wanted out. They played on the blanket. I told my parents about my addiction, and while I looked at my mom for a few seconds—"

"Rose walked somewhere she shouldn't, didn't she?" She wanted to scream. "Is she okay?"

"Both girls are fine. But it was Luna who decided to take her first steps and go right behind the oak tree so I couldn't see her. She's perfectly okay, I promise." His strong hands clasped her arms, as if holding her upright. She hadn't realized her legs were quivering until he steadied her. "She wasn't more than six feet from me, but it was the worst few seconds of my life."

Natalie shut her eyes. "This is my fault. Before you left Foxtail today, I should have reminded you to pay closer attention to them."

"I don't need reminding."

He sounded vexed, but clearly, he didn't understand how serious this was. "It's snake season. Or she could've fallen into a gopher hole or put something dangerous into her mouth, Wyatt."

"Or a million other awful things, but none of them happened."

"Thankfully, but it wasn't because you were watching her."

His hands fell. "That's where we're different, I guess. I may not be wary enough, sure, but your never-ending search for control means you only see potential pitfalls. You miss all the good things along the way."

"It's snake season," she said again.

"You're right. I should've been more aware, but Ranger was calm enough for me to assume there were no threats around, and the girls had been perfectly content to stay on the blanket. If you were there, you might not have executed a search for dangers within a thirty-foot perimeter, either."

She had hurt him. Badly. But didn't he get it? "We must be vigilant, though. Both of us."

"Message received loud and clear." His tone was flat.

"I'm sorry I assumed you were using substances. I went too far, but I hope you can understand why I came to that conclusion."

"I'm understanding a lot right now, that's for sure." Wyatt's frown etched deep lines into his cheeks. "Like how it's only a matter of time before I fail you and the girls. Not because I'm your dad, making promises I have no problem breaking."

Why did he have to bring up her dad? The words stung. "Wyatt—"

"I'm going to fail you because I'm human. I've made mistake upon mistake, for which I am sorry, but none of the things I've done have come from ill intent. Today, looking away from the babies for a moment was an accident. So was not telling you about my business plan until you overheard it from Alex. I should have told you earlier, but I didn't hide it to hurt you."

His reference to that conversation nudged a thought

loose. "I felt like you were hiding something from me that night. It's bothered me since. And when I saw you just now, shaking and agitated, I thought… I'm sorry, Wyatt. Truly, and I hope you can forgive me." Shame spooled in her stomach. "My intuition or gut or whatever you call it was clearly wrong."

"No, Nat, it wasn't. I did withhold something from you." He looked away from her. "Something big."

How many times could her heart stop beating in one conversation? "What?"

His gaze returned to hers. "I'm in love with you. The truth is, I don't think I ever stopped loving you. Not when we drifted apart over a year ago when I turned to a prescription. Not when you removed your engagement ring and told me we were through. Not the times since then when you doubted that I would stay to raise the girls, and not today, when you clearly thought the worst of me."

Her heart pounded in her throat, constricting her breath. He loved her?

"Wyatt, I came here to—"

"But now I know it doesn't matter." He spoke at the same time. "You and my parents have something big in common. I'm not enough for you as I am."

He thought that? "That's not—"

"Love isn't enough, either. Not without trust. And even if you could grow to love me, I'm not sure what it will take for you to ever trust me again."

The world began to spin. "Can you blame me?" Her voice was high, tight. "You looked…compromised."

"I'm not going back to who I was then, Natalie. I understand the reason you came to that conclusion, but this confirms what I always knew in the back of my head. There is no future for us, not in a romantic way. So, when it comes to the girls, we'll draw up a custody agreement, just how you wanted all along. I'll stop the daily commute. I'll stay in Irvine during the week, and I'll come here for the weekends, at least until Alex and I get our business off the ground and I can relocate to Goldenrod. Then, we'll move to a fifty-fifty plan."

It felt as if all the oxygen was leaving the atmosphere. "That's what you want?"

"Don't you? It was your idea. It puts more burden on you for the foreseeable future, I know, and I wanted to avoid that, so I can take them with me to Irvine, if you want."

No, she couldn't bear that. "They're never a burden."

He stared into her eyes, as if waiting for more, but then he shook his head. "Feel free to head back to Foxtail and relax. It's my night with the girls, anyway, but we might as well start the new schedule now. I'll keep them through tomorrow night before I need to leave for Irvine. Can you be at Forrest and Cady's after the girls have their dinner, so I can hit the road?"

Protestations clawed at her throat, but she nodded. "I— Sure."

"We'll meet up at the hearing Wednesday, too, of course." His eyes were dark as ink. "Goodbye, Natalie."

He brushed past her on the path toward the house, leaving her with her hand pressed to her mouth.

What had just happened?

Wyatt loved her, but now he wanted nothing to do with her because she couldn't trust him. He'd given her what she'd wanted all along: an organized, cold plan to raise the girls together without *being* together.

His goodbye said it all. Whatever chance they might have had?

It was over.

Chapter Twelve

The rest of the weekend was terrible.

Not because anything went wrong, exactly. Natalie returned to Foxtail, intending to oversee the wedding cleanup, but Silas and Thatcher had long since cleared the chairs, aisle, arch and flowers. By bedtime, the reception was over, the tent disassembled, the rental chairs and tables loaded back onto a truck, and the caterer's equipment cleared.

Foxtail Farm looked normal again.

Sunday morning, the bride's family checked out of the cabin, raving about their weekend—the wedding, the party and their accommodations. Wyatt would be glad to know how much they'd enjoyed his design, and Natalie appreciated hearing that they would recommend the cabin to their friends. By the end of the day, two sets of guests had booked cabin reservations for summer—both noting on the website form that they had attended Esme's wedding.

But otherwise, Natalie had a perpetual pit in her stomach over her last conversation with Wyatt.

I'm not enough.

Had she, like his parents, expected unrealistic things from him? It was too painful to think about.

Driving to church without him and the girls on Sunday was lonely. She rushed to join them in the pew and hugged the babies tight, but after the service, Wyatt left with Rose and Luna before she had her fill. She drove back to Foxtail alone, hating the quiet.

Don't waste this time to yourself, silly. How many times in the past few months had she wished she had time to curl up with a book? After changing into comfy sweats, she poured boiling water into her favorite mug, dunked a peppermint tea bag into it and curled up on the couch with a thick novel.

Instead of reading, she wondered what Rose and Luna were doing. What Wyatt was doing.

She gave up and went for a walk through the orchard. She popped by the farm stand. She went back to her empty quarters in the farmhouse and ate pistachio ice cream straight out of the carton. The house was too quiet. No baby sniffles or snorts, or the tap-taps of doggy feet on the floor, or Wyatt's low chuckle. No different than the other days and nights she'd had off while Wyatt stayed with the girls, but at the same time, completely, horribly different.

Because this felt final. A sample of the future.

Why had she ever wanted this to be her life?

Eventually, it was time to pack a bag for the week and drive to Forrest and Cady's. Eagerness and anxiety comingled inside her.

"Come on in," Wyatt said as he let her in the front door, his tone as friendly, polite and distant as it had been this morning at church.

"Hey." She stepped around his rolling suitcase, dragging hers into the living room where the twins played on the quilt. "Hello, my darlings."

Seeing her, Luna squealed. Rose broke into a wide smile. "Nee-nee!"

"Is that Natalie? Did you say my name?" Natalie rushed

to them, wishing her arm weren't in a sling so she could hug them both at the same time. "Nee-nee missed you so much." She smooched their heads. Then she felt a warm nudge on her leg, accompanied by loud panting breaths and an unmistakable doggy smell. "Ranger, I missed you, too." She rubbed his neck and back. His mouth opened as if he were smiling.

Behind her, Wyatt cleared his throat.

She turned and their gazes held, tethered as if by magnets. All she wanted was to start over. Blurt something stupid to him, like how much she wanted love to be enough.

Instead, she sat on the floor like a lump on a log while he picked up a sheet of computer paper from the coffee table. "Shall we go over the schedule for the coming week?"

"Sure." She rose and took the paper he held out to her. It was a calendar, with his work commitments entered in tiny font.

"I'm available to you anytime, but I noted meetings where I might not be able to answer my cell immediately, just so you're aware. If you want to add your own appointments to the calendar, the program is loaded on the computer in the office. It's saved to the cloud so we can both access it."

Her organization-loving heart leaped, but not as high as it would have if Wyatt weren't looking as glum as a shriveled apple. "This is a good idea."

"One other thing." He led her into the kitchen. "It's important to keep the lines of communication open in regard to the girls' changing habits and diets and so forth, so I started a few charts. There's one so we don't accidentally repeat their foods. It's on the fridge."

She glanced at it, drawn on grid paper in his neat, architect-trained hand. Apparently, they had eaten green beans and rice for lunch. "You've been busy."

"This page isn't so much a chart as a place to note new habits. Luna crawled more than she walked yesterday, but who knows how long that will last. That's about it. I'll meet you at the courthouse on Wednesday, if that's okay. It's a faster drive for me if I go straight to El Cajon instead of here first."

"Of course. It wouldn't make any sense to come all the way up the mountain and then go down again. We'll see you at ten o'clock sharp."

"It's all settled, then." He returned to the living room and scooped both girls in his burly arms, nuzzling their heads. "Bye, Lu-lu, bye, Rosie. I love you and I'll see you soon."

Luna snuggled into him. Rose patted his stubbled cheek and then reached down, like she wanted to return to her toys. He set them down on the quilt, whistled for Ranger and nodded at Natalie. "See you in a few days."

And then he was gone.

This was how it would be with them from now on.

Passing each other with packed suitcases when they switched houses.

Talking for five minutes or less about the girls' meals and milestones.

No warmth or laughter, just the transfer of information.

Exactly what she'd wanted in the first place.

On Monday, she took the girls to the farm stand, ate a picnic lunch with them on a blanket in the blooming orchard and returned to the house, handling Foxtail business while they napped. Tuesday was spent much the same way, with the lone addition of confirming the next day's guardianship hearing with their lawyer, Mr. Phillips, and mocking up the custodial schedule on paper to take with them to the hearing.

Tomorrow already, Lord? It seemed like a lifetime ago that she and Wyatt first met in Mr. Phillips's office and learned they were named as the girls' guardians. She had been so certain Wyatt would disappoint them that she'd strongly considered giving Rose and Luna up to Forrest's cousins, thinking they might have a safer, more stable life. Now, the idea of parting with them seemed unthinkable.

As darkness fell, Sadie arrived to help with the babies' baths and bedtime bottles. As Sadie gathered clean diapers and pajamas from the girls' room, Natalie pulled out two dresses from the girls' closet to wear to tomorrow's hearing. Not as fancy as the Easter dresses they had already grown out of, but new frocks in cheery red. The hairbows that matched them the best were the apple bows Wyatt had purchased back at the Valentine's Day event for the animal shelter—a memory that was both happy and sad, considering all that had happened since then.

Natalie and Wyatt might not have a future, but they would always be the girls' family. The bows were a tangible reminder of that, so she set them beside the dresses for tomorrow.

"Dove and I want to go with you tomorrow." Sadie's words dragged Natalie from her thoughts. "And before you argue, yes, we really want to come. Yes, we found people to cover us at the farm stand. Does that defuse all your counterpoints?"

"It does, and it means a lot that you'll be there. Thank you."

"Thatcher would come, too, but somebody needs to be on the farm."

"Totally."

"Mick said Wyatt's parents are coming. They're total softies where the girls are concerned."

Maybe someday they would soften in other ways, accepting Wyatt for who he was, not the image he presented on the surface. Not valuing only his successes and victories. Knowing the real him and loving him.

Knowing the real him. Something she hadn't done, either. She hadn't fully accepted him for who he was, who he strove to be with God's help, judging him only on his past and her fears.

That thought stayed heavy on her mind after the girls fell asleep and Sadie returned to Foxtail. Natalie made her way to the living room and curled beneath the crocheted blanket. Listened to the creaks of the house settling. Felt her heart beating, hard and slow in her chest, every beat an ache.

She knew the real Wyatt now…and he knew the real Natalie. The worst parts of her. Her control issues, her fear-based rigidity, her difficulty trusting, all of it.

And cared for her anyway. Loved her anyway.

Enough to work around the clock to care for the girls, finish the gorgeous cabin, help her pull off the wedding, commute out of town to work full-time to the best of his ability and dare to dream of a way to stay in town.

He had made gesture after gesture to show her he was committed to the girls. To her as co-guardians.

When it came to her acquaintance with Wyatt's flaws, however, she'd used them to define him in her mind. She'd made assumptions. Granted, his behavior at Manzanita after the wedding had seemed suspicious, considering his history, and she had the girls to consider. Yet it hadn't taken much for her to assume the worst of Wyatt.

A shrill cry pierced the silence, earsplitting and frantic. Natalie jumped out of her skin, then bolted upstairs.

Rose stood in her crib, screaming, her little fists clutching the guardrail. Natalie scooped up the baby with her good arm, quickly checking that Luna was all right. Awakened, but drowsy, the little one would surely fall back to sleep. Natalie rushed Rose out of the room, down the stairs, back to the light of the living room.

"What hurts, little one?" She laid Rose on the couch and, though it was awkward with her broken arm, she checked her diaper, examined her for rash, felt her forehead and back for evidence of fever, all while the baby arched her back and screamed. This was too intense for a toothache or growing pain. "Lord Jesus, I can't tell what's wrong. Help her, please," Natalie prayed aloud.

Panic welled in her stomach, spreading into her limbs. She had to do something to help this poor child, but what? Urgent care was closed at this hour. That left the emergency room. She should call her sisters to come stay with Luna. She should probably call Wyatt, too—

A memory from the day of the funeral flashed into her brain. Rose had screamed just like this. What happened next? Wyatt noticed her tummy. And then Natalie remembered that Rose required extra care when feeding.

How quickly she had forgotten, probably because it had not been a problem since then. But tonight, Natalie had been preoccupied and anxious when offering Rose her bedtime bottle. What if Rose had gulped too much air?

Natalie lifted Rose into an upright position, awkwardly propping the baby against her as best she could with only one good arm, so she could check Rose's tummy. It did feel a bit fuller than normal. What had Wyatt done to help her back then? Rub vigorous circles on Rose's back and bounce, didn't he? It was worth a try before rushing to urgent care.

Softly singing a children's praise song, she shifted Rose

so she could rub her back. She couldn't bounce and rub at the same time, one handed, but hopefully this would help. The screeching in her ear didn't subside immediately, but it hadn't for Wyatt, either, had it? All she could do was pray for God to help ease the little one's suffering.

With a heave and a hiccup, Rose let loose with a hot stream of spit-up down Natalie's chest. *Thank You, Lord.* Natalie shifted a burp cloth she had previously left on the couch beneath Rose's head and continued patting her back. Rose let out another watery burp, then a whimper before she snuggled into Natalie's chest.

"Is that better, Rosie? I think so, but let's keep on for a while before we put you to bed, shall we?"

She would have to tell Wyatt his trick had worked again, relieving Rose's discomfort. She was grateful God had put that memory in her mind, but she couldn't help but wish Wyatt had been with her tonight. They worked better together.

The top of Rose's head nestled under Natalie's chin. She kissed the baby's downy hair, trusting she would soon sleep but not wanting to put her down just yet. She shifted Rose's position and stood so she could walk, following the night-lights plugged every so often into the walls like a trail to the office, where Wyatt's presence lingered in the faint fragrances of cedar and leather and pencil shavings.

I miss him, Lord.

Natalie's gaze roved over paperwork on the desk, drinking in the sight of his familiar handwriting. It looked like he had made notes on a sketch, and…was this a topographical map of Foxtail Farm?

Natalie peered closer, spying a red ink dot on the map.

It was her favorite spot on the property. The place where the Granny Smith orchard ended and the meadow began, with the view of the mountains to the right. What on earth? She adjusted the papers so she could look at them all. Really look at them.

On one page, he had sketched a house with a wide porch from which to take in the vista. A sunroom at the back, an enormous kitchen and a laundry area behind it, against an attached garage.

In the page's corner, his neat writing listed bullet points.

- *Ample room. Complies with Asa's will. But does she want this?*
- *If so, style okay? Do not go forward without her input.*
- *D, S, T approve?*

Ample room—the house was for her, Rose and Luna, and since it was located on Foxtail property, it complied with her father's will stating she had to reside on-site. Wyatt also clearly planned to consult with her, as well as Dove, Sadie and Thatcher, because Foxtail Farm was theirs, too.

Something about the way he'd written "do not go forward" caught her attention. He had pressed the pencil forcefully, darkening the words as if he were emphasizing them in his mind. Learning from the past to avoid future misunderstandings.

Could she say the same about herself?

She still held tight control over everything—the farm, the girls—to prevent trouble. Yet trouble came anyway.

Micromanaging and clinging to control hadn't brought her much peace, had they? But God offered the peace she craved, along with restoration, healing and help.

She shut her eyes. *Lord, I'm sorry. You're the One who holds the universe together. Not me. Yet I try, don't I?*

Her mind flashed to her Bible reading earlier today, which had listed many who walked in faith in times past. Noah built the ark before the rain fell. Abraham followed God without a road map.

Life with God required faith. Something she didn't have nearly enough of, perhaps, but she knew God didn't love her any less for it. He had sent His Son for imperfect people, not perfect ones. People like her, so scared of being abandoned by the men in her life that she strove to protect herself at the cost of losing everything.

Still cradling Rose, she dropped into the office chair and continued her prayer, talking to God, who loved her more than she could imagine.

Wyatt loved her, too, but what had he said? Sometimes love wasn't enough.

He was correct. Sometimes a person had to prove it. The only way Natalie could think to do that was to relinquish control and take a risk.

Tenderly, slowly, on tiptoes, she carried Rose back to her crib and checked on Luna. Then she returned to the office, picked up her phone and scrolled through it.

Hopefully, Mr. Phillips wouldn't begrudge her a phone call at this hour. She needed a lawyer.

Wednesday morning, Wyatt hooked a finger between his shirt collar and his tie, which felt tight enough to strangle him. The knot had seemed perfect when he left Irvine, but with every passing mile toward the courthouse in eastern San Diego County, his breathing grew more and more strained.

He parked with plenty of time to spare and paced in front of a silver sculpture in the courtyard, gulping the cool April breeze, but it didn't help relieve his anxiety much.

If only he could have brought Ranger with him, but since the Labrador was no longer in service, he wasn't allowed in the court. Wyatt was grateful for Alex taking the dog for the day.

His parents exited the parking structure, grinning. He strode toward them and hugged his mom, pretty in her pink cardigan and floral dress. Then he shook his dad's hand. "I appreciate you making the drive down here. You two look spiffy."

Dad chuckled. "A big occasion like this calls for me to drag my suit out of the back of the closet."

"I'm shocked moths didn't fly out of that old suit." Mom brushed lint off one gray sleeve, then turned to apprise her son. "You look handsome, too. Blue suits you so well."

"Thanks." But his tailored blazer was starting to feel as tight as his tie now. And hot. Hotter every second he waited, clutching the silver gift bag in his hand. Where were Natalie and the girls?

"Is that a guardianship present?" Mom eyed the bag. "For the girls?"

"It's for Natalie, actually."

"And there she is now." Dad looked over Wyatt's shoulder.

Wyatt turned and his breath caught in his throat. Natalie, arm in a sling but heartbreakingly beautiful in a dress of pine green, walked with Sadie and Dove, who pushed the girls in the double stroller.

Hurrying to meet them, Wyatt offered the women brief greetings before squatting down to Rose and Luna's level. It had only been a few days since he had seen them, but he'd missed them so much his chest ached. They looked adorable in their red dresses, white tights and oh, were those the apple hair bows he had bought for them? That day, he'd felt so much joy and hope for the future. Seeing them on the girls, he couldn't help but feel a spark of hope again that someday, somehow, he and Natalie could heal from the wounds of the past.

But today was not about him and Natalie. It was about the girls. "Wow, don't you two look pretty."

"Yi-yit," Rose yelled.

"I love how you say my name, Rosie. And hello, Lu-lu."

"Ya yoo," Luna interjected, kicking her legs happily.

"I think this is a good day, too." He grabbed their tiny, dimpled hands and kissed them, and then rose to his full height. Natalie met his gaze, then quickly looked down, flushing. Did she hate him so much that she couldn't bear to look at him?

"Looks like we're all plenty early for the hearing," Dad murmured. "Mr. Phillips won't be here for another quarter hour."

Natalie tipped her head. "The girls wouldn't mind a little stretch after such a long car ride."

"I saw a grassy area back that way." Sadie gestured. "Shall we go?"

"If you don't mind, I'd like a moment with Wyatt alone." Natalie met his gaze then. And smiled. A real smile, neither strained nor forced, its beauty so radiant he felt immobilized.

And utterly confounded, since their last parting had been so final, emotionally speaking. The possibility of a future together was dead.

No one said anything while Natalie pulled a large manila envelope and a small box from the cargo area behind the stroller seats. Then Sadie snapped to attention. "Have a good talk."

His mom took charge of the stroller. "See you shortly."

Once they were gone, Wyatt felt as awkward as he had when he'd first asked Natalie on a date a million years ago. Unsure how to begin, he thrust the gift bag at her. "This is for you."

"Really? Thanks. Here, hold this." They exchanged the items in their hands, since she couldn't hold everything with her sling. Hooking the bag's handle over the fingers of her right hand, she pulled out a carved, foot-tall wooden cross with her left. Carved, sanded and stained a rich color he hoped she would like. "Oh, my. It's beautiful, Wyatt. You made this?"

"Out of the incense cedar that crashed onto the cottage. There are three more just like it, one each for Dove, Sadie and Thatcher. That tree is part of the Foxtail Farm story, but now, I hope its wood also serves as a reminder that God takes broken things and makes beauty out of them."

Her eyes moistened. "It's taken me a while to see where God has done that in my life, but to be honest, I haven't always been looking. I've missed a lot of things that were right in front of me. Until now."

"What do you mean?"

"I brought something for you, too." She gestured to the items she had brought, still in his grasp. "Open the envelope first."

He wasn't sure he wanted to, if the envelope held what he thought it did. "Is this the custody calendar for the judge to see?"

"Take a peek."

Bracing himself, he tugged the papers out. Then he scanned the document printed on Foxtail Farm letterhead, which Dove, Sadie and Thatcher had all signed.

"Foxtail is offering to stable the Happy Hooves horses? For free?" He looked down into her smiling face. "Why?"

"Don't the mares need a place to stay until your equine therapy ranch is ready?"

"Yes, but I—I don't understand."

Her eyes twinkled in the morning sun. "Remember my dad's will? How my family can't change how Foxtail is run for five years, or we lose it? That means we can't add to the business or develop the fallow property, but Mr. Phillips says we can stable the mares at Foxtail if we don't charge you rent. If we did, it would count as a new moneymaking venture and defy my dad's will. You'll have to provide for the mares' care, of course, and you can move them anytime you find a permanent space. However, if you're willing to wait another four years, when the terms of Dad's will are fulfilled, Foxtail would be happy to donate a sector of property for the ranch."

Wyatt's heart filled his throat. "Your family did all this for me?"

Her family. Not his. She seemed to understand what he meant. "This happened early this morning, so I haven't had time to tell your parents yet," she clarified. "But Sadie texted Mick, and he's thrilled. Willing to donate his veterinary services, too."

That was his cousin—no, his brother. In every way except birth.

Natalie shifted her stance. "Does he know yet why the idea of a therapy ranch is so near and dear to your heart?"

"I planned to tell him this weekend, when I came back for the girls. Thatcher, too. If you haven't told him already."

"It's not mine to tell, so no. Not him, not my sisters."

Wyatt cleared the emotion from his throat. "It means a lot to me that they would support the ranch without knowing why I want to do it."

"We love you, Wyatt."

We. Not *her*, but it was a start toward building a more amicable future, wasn't it?

"I am a blessed man." He shoved thoughts of love, in all its forms, from his head, determined to keep things light. "Now I need to find volunteers willing to care for the horses during the workweek until I can move back to Goldenrod."

Natalie shook her head. "No more out-of-town stuff. I want you to quit your job."

Wyatt couldn't have heard her correctly. "I can't. Not until the business gets off the ground."

"Which is why you need to devote yourself to it fully. There's a demand for the product you and Alex are offering."

"It might not be profitable for a while, though, Nat, and I need to provide for the girls—"

"I can float us for a while. All four of us—you, me and the girls. If you're willing. Open the box now."

Tucking the paper under his arm, Wyatt lifted the lid on the small wooden box. Inside was a blue velvet box that had sat atop his dresser for weeks before he proposed to her.

A wave of shock washed over him. "It's your engagement ring."

"I'm all thumbs, or I would open it. Will you?"

He pried the hinged lip up with a soft snap. Inside, on a bed of blue satin, the solitaire diamond—simple yet elegant, much like Natalie herself—glimmered in the morning sunshine, flickering questions in him.

She knew he loved her. He had told her so, right before he told her goodbye. Why was she doing this?

When he looked down at her, she was smiling. Flirtatiously so.

A slow grin spread on his face as joy lapped from his chest to his fingers and toes. "Why, Natalie Ann Dalton, are you asking me to marry you?"

"I am absolutely not asking you." Her tone was light as cotton candy. "But I'm saying yes again. If you're willing, that is."

He wanted to swoop her into his arms, but she wasn't done talking. "Dutch said something that stuck with me about how partners in a marriage need to give more than fifty-fifty, and I think he's right. I don't want to raise the girls fifty-fifty with you, just like I don't want a relationship that's fifty-fifty. I want to give a hundred percent of myself to the girls and to you, and I want all of you, too. Wyatt, can you forgive me for thinking the worst, time after time?"

"How could I not, when I'm the one who gave you reason to doubt me?"

"I let you down, though. I didn't support you. I made you believe I wouldn't tolerate you if you had any struggles. That's not loving or caring. Or fair, considering I could wear a T-shirt that says 'abandonment issues' on it. I don't want to look at you that way anymore, or view the world as a dangerous place I have to map out so I can avoid trouble. It comes anyway, so I would rather focus on God and see things through His eyes. I trust Him, and I trust you. Not to be perfect, or to never stumble, but to hold fast to God and to me and the girls. To get back up again."

"You trust me?" He had never felt so humbled.

"I can't promise I won't falter sometimes, because I'm human. But I don't just trust you. I love you, Wyatt. Love who you are, all of you. Your heart, your mind, your laugh, your past, present and future. And I want you. Officially, husband and wife, if you'll have me. Or we can leave it as friends, if that's what you—"

"Officially. Definitely. I want it official." Lifting her chin with his thumb, he glanced at her lips, then claimed them. And he might not have stopped kissing her if there wasn't a ring he couldn't wait to put on her finger. "I love you, Natalie. Even more than I did the first time I asked you to marry me. I want to give one hundred percent to you and to the girls. To our family. Will you marry me?"

"Yes, Wyatt. One hundred percent, yes."

He slid the ring on her delicate finger, then hoisted her in the air and swirled her in his arms. "We're going to be a family."

"You, me, Luna and Rose." She was breathless when he set her back on her feet. "And Ranger."

He still held her in his arms, unwilling to let go just yet. "And Happy Hooves, but we're changing the name to something more in keeping with a therapy ranch."

"And Beacon."

"And babies."

She laughed. "I already said the babies."

"No, I mean new ones. I think Rose and Luna would like a brother or sister. Or both."

"Ohhhh." A tinge of pink flushed her smiling cheeks.

"I'm so sorry for interrupting." Wyatt's mom's voice was loud but tentative.

He looked up, holding on to Natalie's hand as their family members approached, eyes wide with curiosity. Mom, however, looked embarrassed, gesturing at the girls in the stroller. The babies' white tights were stained green at the knees. "I'm so sorry. I know how much you wanted to make a perfect impression."

"My definition of perfect has changed." Natalie brushed off his mom's concerns. "I see two happy babies, about to be made official with two committed guardians. Our home, like life, won't be perfect, but it will be full of love—for them, and for each other."

Dove gasped. "Did you say love?"

"For each other?" Mom's gaze flew straight to Natalie's ring finger.

Sadie's hands clasped beneath her chin. "Ha, I knew it."

"That makes one of us," Dad said with an eye roll.

There was much more to discuss. Much more to plan, to dream, to celebrate. But right now, they had an appointment. One that would change their lives forever, for the better.

Wyatt squeezed Natalie's hand. "Let's go inside and make this guardianship official."

Epilogue

One year later

"**W**ait up, Nat. We don't want to mess this up."

Natalie pivoted on the new concrete path dividing the bright sod lawn in two, just steps from the cabin-style, two-story home. Now that the moment had arrived, Natalie didn't want to delay a second longer than necessary. "Mess *what* up? The house you built is finally ready. Inspections are over. We've waited a year for this."

"Forever, actually." Wyatt's hands spanned her waist, pulling her back toward him, dipping into her so his lips landed soft as a butterfly's wing at the base of her neck. "That's how long I've wanted—waited—to carry you over the threshold of our home."

The way he nuzzled her, his warm breath fanning her skin, she forgot how to think. "Isn't the threshold tradition supposed to happen on the wedding day?"

That happy ceremony had occurred six months ago, after the apple harvest. It was a short engagement, perhaps, but they hadn't wanted to wait to get married. Not when they had wasted so much time apart.

Not when they wanted to be a family with Rose and Luna. The past year, almost to the day since they stood in front of the courthouse and declared their love, had been rich in joy and busy with change as they prepared to create a home together, literally and figuratively. Wyatt had begun the process of building their home behind the Granny Smith trees. They'd discussed adoption with their lawyer to make things official with Luna and Rose. And they'd sought counseling with their pastor to ensure their marriage began on the right foot, in step with Jesus.

They'd made individual changes, as well. Natalie had contracted a bookkeeper for Foxtail, a decision that pinched the budget but freed her schedule for more time with the babies. Giving up control of the books hadn't been easy, but it was so worth it.

Wyatt and Alex had taken the plunge starting their new business, Cuyamaca Cabins, and already had so many project requests that they'd had to start a waiting list. The twosome also served on the new board of their nonprofit, Hearts and Hands Ranch, which had found partners to fund the purchase of land. For now, Willard's mares spent their days at the stable on Foxtail property, the horses tended to by future volunteers of the H&H Ranch, including Silas.

Natalie sent up a prayer of thanksgiving for their second chance at a life together. "I'm ready if you are."

His hands shifted, sweeping her off her feet, against his chest. As gorgeous as the new house was, with its white pine log exterior and wide windows, the view six inches in front of her was far more engaging. She cupped his neck and pulled him down for a kiss.

Afterward, he chuckled. "We'll never get onto the porch at this rate."

"All right, all right." She snuggled against his flannel-clad chest as he strode effortlessly up the three steps, crossed the porch and shifted to push open the door.

It took a moment for her eyes to adjust, and then all she could do was gasp. "It's the most beautiful house I've ever seen."

"We're two steps inside. You can hardly see anything yet."

"I don't need to." The hardwood floors in the hall, the plush carpet in the living room ahead, soft enough for the girls to play on, the sun streaming through the rear windows, filling the house with light. It was stunning.

Laughter and voices carried behind them. "They're here." As much as she never wanted Wyatt to put her down, she couldn't wait to greet Rose and Luna, who had been visiting the H&H horses with the rest of the family so Wyatt and Natalie could have a first-look moment alone.

But now, two toddlers with strawberry blond hair— one in short pigtails, the other with loose curls—bounded through the door, their sure, loud steps echoing in the empty hall. Every day, the precious girls reminded Natalie and Wyatt of Forrest and Cady, renewing their commitment to honor their beloved late friends by raising their children with as much love, joy, and happiness as their hearts could hold.

Wyatt set Natalie on the ground, and they each grabbed a twin, kissing cheeks and squeezing tight, as their families— and Ranger—streamed in through the front door.

"Nice job, son." Wyatt's mom stared around in wonder.

"Fine work," Wyatt's dad admitted. "I'm proud of how this turned out."

"It's gorgeous," Dutch murmured, exchanging approving looks with Beatie.

Alex came alongside Wyatt and gave him a fist bump. "We did good, man."

"Hey, I recognize this cross." Dove pointed at the cedar cross hanging by a slim nail on the wall beside the front door.

Natalie reached for Wyatt's hand. "That's the perfect place for it. Thank you."

"I wanted us to see it whenever we came or went. To remind us this house is built on Jesus."

"Ranger likes it here." Mick pointed to the dog, who had curled up in a patch of sunlight beneath one of the living room windows, his tail thumping in a happy beat.

"I do, too," Thatcher added with a laugh. "Where can I sign up for a Cuyamaca cabin?"

"I think we can hook you up," Alex said.

Natalie's gaze met Wyatt's. They didn't need words to understand what the other was thinking. After trials and difficulty, they were home now, at last. He lifted Natalie's hand to his lips for a kiss that was brief but full of promise.

Chatter filled the house as their family and friends toured every nook and cranny. There was no furniture on which to sit for the family gathering. No food in the refrigerator to share. Nothing extra in the house at all, except for the cross fashioned of incense cedar wood, hanging by the front door.

But there was so much love, it surely spiraled out the chimney and spilled out the windows.

* * * * *

*If you enjoyed this story, look for these
other books by Susanne Dietze:*

Seeking Sanctuary
A Small-Town Christmas Challenge
A Need to Protect
The Secret Between Them

Dear Reader,

I hope you enjoyed meeting Wyatt, Natalie and their community in the Cuyamaca (pronounced *kwee-ah-mack-ah*) Mountains in this first book of my new series. Thank you so much for picking up their story! I'm humbled and grateful.

While I was writing, I enjoyed researching what happens to apple trees in winter. Like many other types of plants, they go into a season of dormancy, without which they don't bear fruit. I found a spiritual parallel in my own life, because I was in a prolonged period of winter in my heart. Life takes unexpected turns and sometimes we don't understand why hard things happen, but I learned that God doesn't waste anything. He brings fruit from times of rest, grief or dormancy. Beauty from ashes!

Natalie and Wyatt learned this, too, but it is a lesson I will continue to ponder for some time.

For those seeking information or help fighting substance abuse, the SAMHSA helpline in the United States is 1-800-662-HELP. Additionally, pastors and medical personnel often know of local resources.

To keep up with my book news or giveaways, you can subscribe to my newsletter at https://bit.ly/SusanneDietze-Newsletter, find me at Facebook.com/SusanneDietzeBooks or follow on Instagram.com/SusanneDietze.

Blessings, and thank you for reading!
Susanne